Temporary Nanny for the Tycoon

By Marie Tuhart

Temporary Nanny for the Tycoon

Blake Ellington doesn't need the complication of taking care of his niece in the middle of delicate business negations, but what choice does he have? His mother is in the hospital, and his sister is out of the country. He has no idea how to handle a baby, let alone one that won't stop crying.

When Practically Perfect Nannies sends over Abby Thomas, Blake is thrilled, though the spark between them is disturbing. He doesn't have time for this attraction. It's only for a week. He can avoid the temptation, can't he?

With an outrageous amount offered for the nanny job, Abby will have enough to support herself as she goes after her dream of being a full-time pastry chef. She can't refuse.

She didn't expect to find her client so irresistible, but he is a client, and she has a rule about not getting involved. Besides, she doesn't need a man in her life. Her job is to take care of the baby, and that's what she plans to do. Until Blake kisses her.

ACKNOWLEGMENTS

Laurie, for helping me when I said this book was a hot mess.

To the For Written to Recommended group for all the co-working sessions.

Red Quill Editing, you are the best team to work with.

Publisher's Note: This book contains sexy situations.

To My Readers:

Enjoy my book in the Practically Perfect Nannies world. I had a lot of fun with this story.

Chapter 1

Blake Ellington pulled up to the curb several feet from the fire truck and paramedic unit in front of his childhood home. The engine of his luxury sports car had barely stopped running when he had the car door open and was sprinting up the walkway, his heart thumping hard in his chest.

"Mom?" he yelled as he cleared the doorway. His voice shook with emotion.

"Kitchen." Was her voice frailer than usual? He picked up the pace.

The 70s-style hub of the house he'd grown up in was over-full. Fireman were everywhere, and two paramedics were talking to his mother. Pain etched her face. "What happened?" he asked, trying to control his panic. While his mother wasn't old, she wasn't a spring chicken either.

"All my own fault," Maggie said. "I spilled water earlier, but Katie started crying. When I came back into the kitchen after I got her settled, I slipped and fell."

Blake ran his hand over his face and looked at the two men trying to splint his mother's ankle. "Looks like a bad sprain, maybe a fracture. We're taking her to Swedish, but she refused to leave until you arrived."

"You need to take care of Katie."

Blake approached his mother after they moved her to the stretcher. "I've got it, Mom." He'd do anything so she'd rest and let the doctors do their work.

"Bottles and food in the fridge, diaper bag is in the bedroom, and don't forget her car seat. Do not call your sister. This is the first trip she and Jack have had in years. They need this time alone."

He nodded, stepped away so the paramedics could wheel her out. The firefighters left, and Blake sighed. *What the hell should I do now. I can't go to the hospital and leave Katie here. I can't take her with me. Shit. Wait. Patrick's an orthopedic surgeon. I'll call him.*

Blake checked on Katie, who was asleep in a small round thing. Oh yes, a small looking crib. He picked up the diaper bag and carried it into the kitchen as he called his friend's office. After he talked with Patrick, who assured him he would go to the ER to check on Maggie, Blake pulled the bottles and food out of the fridge and put them in the bag and zipped it shut.

There was no way he could stay at his mother's. He still had his job to do, and her internet could be spotty at times. Worry made his hands twitch as he picked up the diaper bag. It would be okay. Patrick would call him soon.

He carried the diaper bag and package of diapers to his car, switched the car seat base out from his mother's car to his. After twenty minutes of swearing and off-the-scale aggravation, he finally got the thing properly installed. No one ever needed to know he'd had to google how exactly to do it. Who knew they were so hard to fasten in? Back inside, he listened. Katie was still sleeping. Good. He found the carrier that fit into the car seat base and took it into the bedroom.

Gently, he lifted Katie out of the bed. The baby wiggled, and he froze. When she stilled, he put her in the seat and fastened her in. He tiptoed with the carrier to the front door, quietly locking it, and froze when the lock clicked a little too loudly. He glanced down at the baby, still sleeping. He let out a breath.

Carefully, he placed Katie in the car. She looked like a little angel with soft blonde hair. He shut the door with infinite care, raced around to his side of the car, and slipped inside. Was the door latch always so loud? Blake froze again as Katie whimpered, then slipped back into sleep. He drove home so slowly, it took twice as long to get there.

The trip gave him time to think. If his mother just sprained her foot, she'd come home in a few hours. He could bring her back to his apartment. If she broke it…it would take a lot longer to heal.

But she wouldn't be able to watch Katie. How the hell would he get his mother home with a baby to care for? He'd worry about it later. Sure, his apartment wasn't child proof, but she was so little. She wouldn't be able to get into anything.

Besides, how hard could it be, taking care of a ten-month-old?

* * * *

Abby Thomas pushed her hair away from her face Monday morning. "Done," she declared and sat back in her chair with satisfaction. She was finished with culinary school and was now a pastry chef on top of it. It had taken a while, but she'd pursued her dream and achieved it without going into debt.

Between her nanny job, weekends working at a bakery, and occasional restaurant work, she was ready to get out into the world. Well, almost. She'd have to find a balance between the nanny job and restaurant work. She'd already found several openings in the Seattle area and would apply this week.

Her cell rang, and she frowned when she saw *Practically Perfect Nannies Seattle* on the screen.

"Hey, Irene. Did you forget I'm off this week?" Abby stood and stretched. It was barely nine in the morning, but Abby had been up since six.

"I didn't, and I'm calling because I need you."

"Irene…" Abby started.

"I know I promised you this week off, but you're my only hope. A client just called in full panic mode. He needs a 24/7 nanny now. You're the only one qualified who isn't already on a job. It's just until Sunday. I'll give you next week off."

Abby sighed. She didn't like the idea of letting her boss down, but she needed this week off to apply for jobs and go on interviews. "Irene—"

"He's willing to pay four times you're going rate."

Abby's jaw dropped open. "Four times?" she whispered and did a quick calculation in her head. Even with the agency's cut, she'd make more in one week than she did in a month or more. While she really wanted the week off, the money would help her quit her job as a nanny and devote her time to becoming a full-time pastry chef.

"Yes, four times. What do you say?"

"Are you taking your usual percentage?"

"Honey, I'm desperate. I'll knock ten per cent off the agency portion if you'll do this for me."

"Give me all the information."

* * * *

Abby pulled her little compact car up to the call box at the gated garage. Monday traffic hadn't been too bad, so she arrived sooner than anticipated. The client's name, Blake Ellington, bounced around in her head. The name sounded familiar, but she couldn't place it. She was in one of the more exclusive areas of Seattle. She pressed the button on the box.

"May I help you?" came a male voice.

"Yes, hi, I'm Abby from Practically Perfect Nannies. Mr. Ellington is expecting me."

"Oh yes, Ms. Thomas. If you'll pull into slot fifteen and take the elevator to the lobby, I'll meet you there."

"Thank you." The gate rose, and Abby parked in number fifteen. She grabbed her backpack out of the backseat, and pulled her suitcase from the trunk. She glanced at the expensive sports cars, SUVs, and other vehicles as she made her way to the elevator.

When the doors opened at the lobby, a young man in a suit stood there. "Ms. Thomas, I'm Walter, the concierge."

"Please call me Abby." The lobby was all chrome and reflective surfaces. The soft plush looking sofa groupings screamed high end.

He nodded. "Mr. Ellington is anxious for your arrival. We'll take the other elevator." He gestured to her suitcase. "Do you need some help?"

"No, I'm fine. Thank you." A concierge? Blake Ellington must be rolling in the money to afford a place with a concierge. She sighed. A vision of her mother chasing wealthy men danced in her head. She shoved the thought away with a barely perceptible shudder. Don't judge by what you're seeing, she reminded herself.

She followed Walter to the other elevator. Once inside, he slid a card key into the slot, pressed the button for the twentieth floor. "This card key gives you access to the elevators and to Mr. Ellington's apartment."

"Thank you." Abby accepted the card. While technically Mr. Ellington hadn't formally hired her yet, based on the urgency, she assumed it was a done deal and slipped the card into her pocket. Security was tight here. Well, that was expected in a place like this. No wonder this man could afford to pay her four times the normal amount. The elevator pinged, and the doors opened.

Her feet sank into the luxurious beige carpet when she stepped out. Walter escorted her to number twenty-one. "Just put the card key up to the reader, and the door will unlock."

Abby pulled the card out and did what he said. There was a soft buzz, and he turned the handle. The second the door opened, a baby's screams could be heard. Oh no. The baby was not happy.

"I'll leave you here. If you need anything, just dial 2-

4 on the phone. That will ring me." Walter beat a hasty retreat.

Abby chuckled. Experience had taught her most men preferred to run from crying babies rather than solve the problem. Abby stepped into the apartment and set her suitcase and backpack by the door. "Mr. Ellington?" She raised her voice. "I'm Abby, here from Practically Perfect Nannies."

"Thank God." A disheveled man walked into the room with the crying baby in his arms.

His dark hair—Abby would bet her salary it was usually perfect—stood out in all directions. He was wearing…a white button-up shirt? It was hard to tell beyond all the baby spittle and…green beans? The first three buttons were undone, and she caught a glimpse of chest hair before he marched over to her. "Take her." He thrust the baby at her.

Without second thought, Abby took the baby. "Oh sweetheart, what's the matter?" Blue eyes stared at her, then the wailing started once again.

"How long has she been like this?" Abby asked.

"Since last night. I can't take it anymore. I haven't

slept in over a day, and I have a meeting"—he glanced at the watch on his wrist—"at five this evening with my group in Hong Kong. I'm going to bed." He reached into his pocket and pulled out a card and handed it to her. "If you need anything, just order it. I have no idea what a baby needs."

Abby took the card, a little dumbfounded. Without another word, he turned and marched into what she assumed was his bedroom and closed the door. The baby hiccupped. "Well, sweetheart, I guess I'm hired, and it's just you and me. Let's see if we can figure out what's making you cry." And Abby noticed the smell. "Okay, step one. Clean diaper."

There was a diaper bag on the counter, Abby cradled the baby against her and pulled out the lone diaper and wipes. "I don't think your daddy is prepared. Let's see how we can do this." Keeping the baby against her shoulder with her hand under her butt and the other on her back, Abby walked around the well-appointed condo until she found another bedroom. This must be where she would stay.

The room was decorated in nice neutral colors, and

there were no signs anyone lived in it. The bed would work for now. Making a quick detour to the bathroom, she grabbed a couple of towels and placed them on the bed, and laid the baby down. She was surprised to see the baby wasn't in 2-piece footie jammies. Come to think of it, there were no clothes in the diaper bag. She quickly undressed the baby, and saw the issue. Thank goodness she hadn't taken the diaper off yet.

"You need a bath, young lady." Wrapping the towel around the baby and diaper, she walked into the bathroom. No tub. The sink was too small. Okay. Grabbing a couple more towels and throwing them over her shoulder, Abby made her way to the kitchen.

"Yeah, Daddy certainly wasn't prepared for you." Why was he so unprepared? An absent father maybe, and mom needed a break? The baby whimpered. The kitchen sink would do. Turning on the water, she began to sing softly to the baby, whose name she assumed was Katie, since the name was embroidered on the side of the diaper bag. Once the water was warm, she took off the diaper.

"Oh damn," she whispered. The poor baby. There was poo everywhere. No wonder she was crying. "It's okay, sweetheart. Abby will make you feel better." Cradling the baby over one arm she slid her bottom under the water, still humming.

Instantly, the crying stopped. "I know. Daddy had no clue, did he?" Gently she washed Katie, made sure she was totally clean, then laid her on a clean towel. Katie waved her arms in the air as Abby applied some lotion she found in the diaper bag to the baby's bottom and put the last diaper on her.

She placed Katie on the pristine tiled floor while she rolled up the soiled diaper and opened the cabinet under the sink. "Phew." She tossed the diaper in the garbage and shut the door. "You, young lady, know how to smell a place up."

Abby picked up the now quiet baby and went into the living room. One glance around told her this was no place for a baby. She estimated Katie was between eight and ten months old. The tables were glass with sharp edges, plus she couldn't find any baby clothes, let alone any toys or a place to put the baby.

She pulled the card out of her pocket. Well, if Daddy was loaded, this wouldn't hurt too much. She hoped. First step, get some diapers and baby furniture here. Everything else could wait for a half hour or so. Cradling Katie, Abby pulled her cell phone out and made a call. Crib, playpen and high chair from a rental place the agency dealt with all the time.

Katie was much calmer now. Abby pulled the comforter off her bed and placed it on the floor and laid the baby on it. A laugh floated in the air, and Abby grinned. Abby quickly grabbed her backpack and pulled out her computer.

Sitting on the floor with her computer on the glass coffee table, she opened her laptop. She could sit here, get items ordered, and watch Katie. Luckily, Abby knew all the places she could order where they could make deliveries within hours.

She glanced over to see Katie had fallen asleep. What a little angel. Katie was probably tired, especially since she'd been crying for most of the night. Now clean, she'd gone out like a light.

Within in an hour, Abby had everything ordered for Kate. Well, at least the basics. But what about food? Carefully, she stood and made her way into the kitchen and opened the fridge. Almost empty except for a few bottles and jars of baby food. A grocery delivery was next on the agenda.

Once she placed the order, she called Walter and told him about all the deliveries. He assured her he would take care of it. She also told him the baby was sleeping so to be quiet when he escorted the delivery people to the apartment.

Abby looked at the total for everything and felt a momentary pang of guilt about the amount, but it had to be done. This was for Katie.

A dad who was completely clueless about taking care of his baby. She'd seen it all, but something told her this was going to be an interesting seven days.

Chapter 2

Blake rolled over and picked up his cell phone. Three-thirty in the afternoon. At least he'd finally gotten some sleep. He noticed he had a text from Patrick. He'd called the doctor, thinking maybe his mother was being released. After a fifteen minute conversation with Patrick, who'd taken over his mother's case, Blake was told it would be a week or more before his mom came back home. She hadn't broken her foot, but Patrick wanted her to rest and take it easy, so they were transferring her to a specialty care unit that took care of issues like this. Patrick reassured him his mother was doing just fine and would recover nicely.

Climbing out of bed, he stopped and listened. Silence. He wasn't sure if that was a good thing or not. Striding nude to the bathroom, he turned on the shower and stepped in.

Once he was done, he dressed in the suit he needed for his meeting. He was meeting with the Hong Kong group at eight Tuesday morning for them—five in the evening Monday night for him—and he had a reputation to uphold.

He opened his bedroom door. His apartment was silent. He stepped out and stared. Katie was in some sort of pen, smiling and happy. The nanny was sitting on his light brown sofa folding clothes. The corners of all the tables in the living room had been covered with something, and there was a high chair next to the dining room table.

"Feeling better, Mr. Ellington?" the nanny asked as she continued to fold clothes.

"Yes." He moved to Katie. "How are you, Miss Katie?"

The baby cooed at him instead of crying. Blake released a breath, turned to the woman sitting on the sofa.

He'd barely glanced at her when she arrived. Now he studied her. Her blonde hair was pulled back into a ponytail, and the light blue t-shirt with the words *Practically Perfect Nannies* sprawled across was tucked into a pair of tan pants. He hadn't expected such a stunning woman as a nanny.

"You're a miracle worker." The words slipped from his mouth. This woman had worked some sort of magic in the five and a half hours he'd slept.

"Not really." She glanced up at him. "You were not prepared for Katie, were you?"

"No."

The nanny frowned at his words.

"I'm sorry; I don't remember your name." He was lucky he remembered his. Katie's constant crying had scrambled his brains.

"Abby Thomas."

He nodded. "Ms. Thomas."

"Abby, please." Katie squealed and bounced in her play pen.

"You've been busy." Blake sat down on the sofa, taking in the pile of clothes.

Abby ducked her head. "Poor Katie needed everything, and you did say to get whatever I needed." There was a little bit of laughter in her voice.

"That I did." He didn't care how much she'd spent. It was a drop in the bucket, and Katie was happy now. He kept his gaze on Abby. Her laughter skirted over his skin.

When had someone's laugher been attractive to him? He shook his head. Technically, she was an employee. He'd have to think on it; there were loopholes everywhere.

"The crib, play pen, and high chair are all from a rental company. I did have to buy her clothes, diapers, toys, and I took the liberty of ordering food, not only for Katie but for us as well."

"I had no idea she'd go through all her clothes." Blake shook his head. Sunday afternoon and night had been a crash course in diapers and clothing. At eleven, he'd called the concierge and asked them to run out and get diapers. When they asked him the size, he had no idea. Luckily, when he told them how old Katie was, they knew what to get.

"I'm wondering what you fed her yesterday?"

Blake frowned. "Some of her baby food, a bottle." He paused, thinking back. "While I was trying to eat, she kept reaching from my food, so I gave her some broccoli."

"I see."

"Did I do something wrong? Katie seemed super hungry."

"You said you gave her some baby food and a bottle.

I'm guessing she's between eight to ten months old."

"Ten months." At least he knew that.

"At ten months, they need more than a little bit of food and a bottle. They eat three main meals, a couple of snacks, and three to four bottles."

"I had no clue." He resisted the urge to run his fingers through his hair.

"That's why you called Practically Perfect Nannies."

Thank goodness his mother had put the business card in the diaper bag. He'd found it late last night but couldn't call until eight this morning. When he was told there was no one available, he'd bargained the only way he knew how—with money.

"I'm glad you were able to take the job." Money talked, and apparently, this nanny was no different from anyone else in that respect.

"I was off schedule, but Irene was panicked."

More like afraid of missing out on a healthy paycheck. Blake shook his head. He had to stop that. Not everyone was motivated by money. But in the last few years, he'd found people were often more interested in his money than in him.

His cell rang, and he looked at the screen. "Excuse me, I have to take this."

* * * *

Abby stared at Blake's back. When she'd first seen him all disheveled, she'd noted how good he looked, but in a full suit? Devastating. Handsome didn't begin to cover those intense hazel eyes, perfect cheek bones, or begin to convey the man's sexiness.

She watched him as he chatted on the phone. His voice was low. She recalled where she knew the name from. Blake Ellington, the star subject of the *Washington Inquirer*. It was a gossip rag, but it was fun to read. And Blake Ellington was one of their regular targets.

"Playboy Extraordinaire," the headlines screamed. Yep, seemed to sum him up all right. Abby finished folding the clothes. She didn't do playboys. Heck, she didn't date very much; she didn't have the time. But after her childhood, rich playboys were off the table. She didn't need their kind of trouble in her life. Besides, he was her employer and off limits no matter what.

Glancing at Katie having fun in the playpen dimmed her sour thoughts and made Abby smile. She was really a happy-go-lucky baby. After she'd been cleaned up, fed, and had taken a nap, she'd been great. Abby stood with the baby clothes and walked into her temporary bedroom.

She put the clothes into the empty dresser and glanced around. It wasn't a bad room to spend time in. It had a queen size bed, a TV, along with good lighting, plus a chair with ottoman. And now, a crib. Abby had quietly put her things away—not that she had much—while Katie slept.

Jeans, several Practically Perfect Nanny T-shirts in different colors, other T-shirts, a couple of sleep shirts, and underwear. When she explored earlier, she found a washer and dryer in the apartment. The apartment was good sized. There were at least two bedrooms and another room where the door closed. A full sized kitchen, a small dining area, and a large living room. What she loved was the open air feeling in the living room, dining, kitchen area.

There was a breakfast bar between the kitchen and dining area gave a perception of space and not feeling so closed in. It allowed her to keep an eye on Katie while she was in the kitchen

Back in the living room, she saw Blake staring out the window. His hands were in his pockets, his back straight, but his shoulders were slightly slumped. She wondered if he was wrestling with a problem. She closed her eyes against the perfect masculine figure. She was here to work.

A toy flew out of the playpen. "No, Katie," Abby said in a soft but firm voice. "We don't throw our toys." She picked the toy up and set it on the table, bent over and picked Katie up.

When she glanced at Blake, she noticed his gaze had shifted to her. Until his phone beeped.

"I need to get ready for my call. My office is there." He pointed to the closed door next to what Abby was pretty sure was his bedroom since that's where he disappeared earlier to sleep.

"Go take your call. We'll be fine." Abby smiled and was happy when he disappeared behind the door. "Well, Miss Katie, I don't know about you, but your daddy isn't in full father mode yet. I wonder where your mother is? Not that it's any of my business."

Katie cooed in her arms, and Abby nuzzled her neck, making raspberry noises. "Let's go find you some dinner and a bottle. I know you're still tired."

* * * *

"Earth to Blake," his CFO said.

Blake shook his head. He was supposed to be paying attention to this call; instead, his mind was on Abby. When he'd turned from the window as she bent over to pick up Katie… His libido went crazy.

He really hadn't expected a nanny who was young, pretty, and would raise his blood pressure. "Sorry. I'm a little distracted."

Jeff, his CFO, laughed. "The client seems happy. We should have this one wrapped up within the next two weeks."

"Good." Blake rubbed the back of his neck. His negotiations with the company in Hong Kong had been long and tortuous, but they were nearing the end. "Everything set up to implement once we have the signatures?"

"Yes. I have everyone and everything on standby."

"That will make things easier. Anything else?" The call with the group in Hong Kong had ended twenty minutes ago.

"No. Your assistant said you're working from home

this week?"

"Yeah, Mom had a small accident, and I'm watching Katie."

Jeff burst out laughing. "Who did you hire?"

Blake couldn't help but grin; Jeff knew him well. "Someone from Practically Perfect Nannies."

"Is she cute?"

Blake refused to answer, and it was enough to set Jeff off on a full out guffaw. "Explains the distraction better. Look, I can take care of things here in the office and only bug you as necessary."

"Thanks. There are still a lot of things I need to take care of personally, but I'll shuttle anything that doesn't need my attention to you."

He signed off and sat back in his leather chair. It had been quiet in the apartment the entire call, and Blake wondered if everything was okay. He stood and stretched. Time to get out of this suit and check on Katie and Abby. Opening the door between his bedroom and office, he slipped in and removed his tie and jacket.

The apartment was totally silent when he moved into the living room. The pen where Katie had been before was empty, and he didn't see Abby anywhere. He frowned.

"Abby," he called.

"Not too loud." He turned at the sound of her voice. She slipped out of the spare bedroom, leaving the door cracked. "Katie is sleeping."

"At?" He glanced at his watch. "It's not even seven."

"With the rough night last night, she needs the extra sleep. Did you need something?"

Her words sent a shockwave of awareness through his body. Blake closed his eyes and opened them. "No. It was so quiet, I was concerned."

"There shouldn't be any issues tonight, and I'm here." She turned to go back into the bedroom.

"Did you eat?" He didn't want her to leave. The thought surprised him. He enjoyed his usual solitude, but tonight, he wanted to be with her.

"A little bit. I left a note for you on the kitchen counter." Her hand still gripped the doorknob.

"Would you eat with me?"

Her eyes widened in surprise. "I guess. Let me get the baby monitor." She slipped back into the bedroom.

Baby monitor? What the hell was that? Blake made

his way into the kitchen. It smelled heavenly. Had Abby cooked? Picking up her note he read it: *Casserole in oven, it should still be hot. Sliced bread on the counter, butter in fridge. Not sure what you like to drink, so there's water, soda and beer in the fridge.*

Didn't nannies just take care of the kid? He opened the fridge and pulled out a bottle of water. Abby entered the kitchen with a small white box in her hand. She set it on the counter. "Baby monitor," she remarked when she caught him staring at it.

"What would you like to drink with dinner?" he asked.

"Water is fine." She moved across the kitchen and opened a drawer. After slipping on two potholders, she opened the oven and took out a red and white dish.

"I didn't know a casserole could smell so good." He remembered the tuna casseroles his mother fed him as a kid. Not his favorite dish.

"If you know how to make one, it can be very delicious." She reached up and pulled out plates, and he grabbed utensils and napkins before taking the plates from her.

"I'll put this all on the table while you bring in the

food.”

She nodded. Blake was more than intrigued by this woman. From what he'd seen, she was great with Katie. Setting the table, he waited until she entered. She had a salad bowl balanced on her arm and held the casserole dish. He watched her expertly set the casserole dish on the table and the salad.

“No broccoli,” she said.

Blake laughed and held her chair out for her.

Shock crossed her face, and Blake hid a smile. One thing ingrained in him since childhood: Being a gentleman was important. Maybe he hadn't been so much of one when she first arrived. Katie crying for hours on end had fried every one of his nerves. Now he was well rested and wanted to find out more about Abby.

She dished up what looked like some sort of chicken and pasta before handing him the pan with the potholder underneath. Blake dipped the spoon and scooped some of the food out. Yep, chicken, pasta, green beans, and other things he couldn't readily identify. His stomach growled. It smelled so good.

He picked up his fork, took a bite, and his eyes grew

wide. "This is fantastic. I'm not normally a fan of casseroles."

"It's all in the spices." Abby's lips turned up.

"Care to share what's in it?"

"Besides the chicken, pasta, and green beans?"

"Yes, please." He took another bite, savoring the flavors on his tongue even if he wasn't sure what they were.

"The sauce is a light white cream sauce with basil, bay, garlic, rosemary, tarragon, and thyme. Oh and a dash of paprika."

"It's very flavorful."

Abby nodded. "I made it to be."

"Do you cook a lot when you take care of kids?"

"Sometimes. Depends on who I'm working for and what I'm tasked to do. I know you didn't ask, but we both need to eat, and it's no bother for me to cook." A frowned marred her forehead.

"It's fine." The last thing he wanted was for her to worry he was angry. "I usually go out or have something delivered, so this is a treat." Her features lightened, and he grinned.

"This was simple to throw together. You had the spices in your kitchen."

"I did?" News to him.

A soft laugh floated over to him, and he stared at her. "Yes, you did. Since you confessed to going out or having delivery, I have a feeling you have no clue what's in your cupboards."

He shook his head. She was right; he didn't. "I've only lived here about a year now."

"While eating out can be good, too much of it can cause problems."

"I'm careful." He was touched by her concern, but he was well aware of his eating habits and was slowly making changes.

"I'm sure you are." She ducked her head and continued to eat.

"So what else do you have planned for us to eat this week?" He was curious.

Her eyes lit up, and he was glad he'd asked. "I'm not sure what you like. I have eggs, ham, bacon—all the breakfast foods. I figured on spinach omelets for tomorrow morning, chicken salad for lunch, and steaks, baked potatoes, and corn on the cob for dinner."

His mouth started to water.

"I'm hoping you have a grill. If not, I can do them on the stove."

"I do have a grill." He gestured to the balcony. "It's small and hasn't been used in a while. I'll check it after dinner to make sure we have propane for it."

"Thank you. Should I have breakfast ready at a specific time?"

"What time do you normally eat?"

She wrinkled her nose. "Depends. Katie will want food when she gets up tomorrow, so it will take me about an hour to get her fed and settled. I'm not sure what time she wakes up on a normal day."

"I don't either." Maybe he should call his mom and ask? No, he wanted her to rest. The doctor had told him they wouldn't need to do surgery on her foot, but it was in a boot, and she would be on painkillers for at least the next few days. Plus, they had moved her to the specialty unit, and he wasn't sure about their visitation rules.

Blake had already made arrangements for an in-home aide when his mother was discharged. She was going to be in the boot for two to three weeks. He could already hear her arguing with the doctors.

"I can play tomorrow by ear. What time do you need to be to work?"

"I don't have any meetings until ten. I usually get up around six, go down to the gym, shower, and go to work. While Katie is here, I'll work out of my home office."

Abby nodded, and almost as an afterthought, Blake noticed her cheeks were pink. Interesting.

"A workable schedule."

"How did you become a nanny?"

"A friend in college told me about it."

He tilted his head, staring at her. "I'm sure there's more to the story."

"Yes, but I'm not sure why you want to know."

"Maybe I'd like to get to know the woman taking care of Katie."

Abby bit her lower lip, and shrugged. "Practically Perfect Nannies can give you my credentials if you need them." She pushed back from the table. "If you're done, I'll put the food away and put the dishes in the dishwasher."

He nodded, and she picked up the casserole dish. Blake wondered why she didn't want to talk about herself. In his experience, women loved talking about themselves. He gathered up the rest of the items on the table and carried them into the kitchen.

When Abby bent over to put the casserole in the fridge, his gaze settled on her ass. Damn, the woman was a looker. He'd expected some frumpy older woman, not a young, pretty girl. *Mind out of the gutter, buster. She's here for Katie.*

"I didn't mean to upset you," he said softly as he set the plates in the sink.

"You didn't." She straightened and closed the refrigerator door. "I figured you knew my credentials before you asked for a nanny."

He probably would if he'd been a normal dad hiring a someone to help with his kid. Once again, Blake was struck by how completely unprepared he'd been to take Katie on. Thank God Abby had shown up. "It was kind of an emergency, and I was given the name to call."

"I can understand you weren't prepared." She scooted by him to the sink and rinsed off the plates.

"I wasn't." Understatement of the year. Abby loaded the dishwasher and turned it on.

"If that's all, I'm going to my room." Abby picked up the baby monitor. Who knew there was such a thing?

"Good night." While he wanted to talk with her, he had a feeling he wasn't going to get any more out of her tonight. So Blake let her go and watched as her fine-looking backside disappeared into the spare bedroom.

"Night."

Funny how he hadn't heard a peep out of Katie while they ate. Interesting how Abby made the difference. Instinct told him she was honest and the real deal. Blake's ability to assess people was one of the factors made his business the success it was, and that intuition told him Abby was hiding something.

* * * *

Abby sighed as she closed the bedroom door behind her. She checked on Katie. The little angel was sound asleep with her fist in her mouth.

When Blake started to question Abby, all she heard were the doubts from her childhood creeping back in.

"What makes you think you're good enough?"

"You can't take care of yourself, let alone your brother and sister."

"The house is a mess; clean it up."

She remembered seeing his face and name while in line at the grocery store a few months ago, thinking what a shame such a handsome man lived the life he did. She didn't need a man like him in her life. Her mother had gone through men like they were tissues, swearing they were her ticket out of poverty.

"Right, Mom." Her mother would tell her about each of her playboy boyfriends, but after a few months of attention—less if they found out she had three kids—they would leave.

Abby shook her head. No more looking back. Her brother and sister were doing fine; Abby had seen to that. It was one of the reasons she'd taken the nanny job. Not only could she get her dream job without major school debt, but she had been able to help put her sister through college. Pride coursed through her at how well Libby had done. She was about to graduate summa cum laude and without much debt. Abby had helped make it happen, but the work had been all Libby's.

Her phone pinged, and she smiled when she glanced at the screen. She swiped her finger over the screen. "Hi, Libby," she whispered, greeting her sister on video chat.

"Hi Abby. How's the new job going?"

"Good."

"Oh boy, I hear a but."

Abby laughed. "I wasn't expecting the chaos."

"Sounds interesting. What happened?"

Abby told her about Katie and her day.

"Is the father cute?"

"Libby." Abby tried hard not to smile. "You know I don't talk about the families."

"Okay. I won't ask any more."

Yeah, right. "How is life in New York?"

Abby was glad when her sister began talking about her life. She didn't want to talk about Blake. He was a playboy, the pond scum of the earth, so not a man she should be thinking about.

When she hung up with her sister, Abby grinned. She'd been so lucky with her siblings. Libby and Rob turned out to be great kids. Rob was currently somewhere overseas with the military. She hadn't been surprised when he said he wanted to go in the military instead of college. Rob had a knack for electronics, and the military suited his need for order. Something she'd worked hard to give them as kids. Something their mother hadn't bothered with.

After changing her clothes, Abby climbed into bed, noting the soft feel of the sheets. So much different than hers. Abby shook off the thought. She didn't need material things. She had her brother and sister and, soon, her dream job. The last ten years had paid off, and after this job, she'd have more than enough to go for what she really wanted.

A small cry had her jumping from the bed.

Katie shifted in her crib. Abby checked the diaper. Still dry. Probably just dreaming, but just in case, Abby grabbed her tablet and sat down in the chair to read for a while. Maybe the book would keep her mind off of Blake Ellington.

No such luck.

Chapter 3

The smell of fresh coffee greeted Blake when he entered his apartment the next morning after his workout. He greeted Abby as he stepped into the kitchen. "Good morning."

"Morning." Abby was making something on the stove.

"Our breakfast?" He eyed the white mush.

"For Katie. Want a bite?" She held the spoon out to him.

Blake took a step back, and she lifted the spoon to her lips. "See. Healthy." Abby grimaced, then laughed. "Though not very tasty.

He grabbed mug from the cabinet and poured himself some coffee. "I'm guessing I have time to shower."

"Plenty. It's going to take a half-hour or more depending on how cooperative Katie is."

"Perfect." On his way out of the kitchen, he stopped

by Katie, who sat in her high chair playing with a ring of plastic keys. "Good morning, Miss Katie." He leaned down and kissed the baby on the top of her head.

Katie cooed and laughed at him. At least no more crying, thank goodness. Hiring Abby had been the best thing. Abby set a bowl on the table and moved the chair so she was sitting sideways, facing Katie. Katie pounded the tray of the high chair.

"Okay, Miss Impatient." Abby put some of the oatmeal on a spoon and touched it to her lip before feeding it to Katie.

"Why did you touch the food to your lip?"

"To make sure it isn't too hot."

Something else he didn't know. Blake shook his head. He wasn't cut out to be a father, an uncle sure, but he wasn't going to have kids. He'd seen the heartache his mother had gone through when his father left. His life wasn't conducive to children anyway. He preferred his freedom. Without a word, he left the pair and walked into his bedroom, but the image of Abby feeding Katie stayed with him.

By the time he finished his shower and got dressed, he

was frustrated he couldn't get the image of Abby out of his head. What would her baby look like? Her or its father? Blake banished the image. It wasn't like him to be this distracted.

He made his way into his office and glanced at his calendar. Three calls today, but none of them were major. Maybe he'd have Jeff take the calls for him. Jeff mentioned he'd take the extra workload. Blake stiffened. What was he thinking? He didn't slack off from work. He never had, and he wasn't about to start now. Having a kid and a good looking woman around was messing with his brain.

He needed to get his head back in the game. The first meeting wasn't until ten. It was a little after eight, so he had time. Empty coffee mug in hand, he strode out of his office into the living room area to find Katie in her play pen, laughing.

The aromas of frying bacon and toast made his mouth water. After another glance at Katie, he followed the scent to the kitchen. "It smells good in here."

Abby jumped.

"Sorry, didn't mean to startle you."

"I didn't hear you come in." She glanced over her shoulder at him. "I changed my mind about the omelets. I hope bacon, scrambled eggs, and toast are good for you."

"Whatever you fix is more than welcome. And much tastier than the power bar I usually have." He wasn't used to having someone to cook for him. This was a nice change. He poured himself another cup of coffee. "Can I do anything?"

"If you want to put napkins and utensils on the table."

He nodded as she expertly flipped the bacon over and turned her attention to the eggs. "Do you want me to pour you some coffee?"

"No, thank you. But if you'd grab me a bottle of water, I would be appreciated."

"Sure." Her tone was so formal. Blake shrugged and carried everything out of the kitchen to the small dining area. He set the table, including a bottle of water for Abby and a glass. Before he could return to the kitchen, she walked out with a plate in each hand, and a plate of toast resting on her forearm. "Let me." He reached for the toast, and she froze.

Was she afraid of him? It didn't make sense. They'd

had a pleasant dinner last night. He grabbed the plate of toast and placed it on the table. Abby set his plate down and hers before taking her seat.

"Did I do or say something wrong?" he asked as he sat down.

"What? No. I had everything balanced, so your offer startled me."

He nodded. "You seem tense today."

She rubbed her forehead. "I'm not used to having someone help me."

He wanted to believe that was it, but there was something more. What would make her freeze when he reached for the plate? Abuse? His hackles rose. If it were the case, he'd make sure she understood he would protect her. His need to keep her safe surprised him. He'd just met her yesterday. His stomach growled. He'd figure it out later. Right now, his attention was focused on breakfast.

Katie cooed and kept a running baby commentary as they ate. "I didn't realize babies were so chatty."

Abby laughed, and he enjoyed the sound of her laughter compared to other women. Her laugh was low key and musical; other women he'd met laughed with a high pitch, almost like a whine.

"Some more than others. How much have you been around Katie?"

"Not too much. Her mother doesn't come here often. She had an event out of the country, and Katie's normal caretaker injured herself, so I was called." The doctor had called him this morning to let him know his mother was settled in the new unit and doing fine, and he could call her. Knowing his mother, she'd want him to come visit with Katie. He wondered if he could do it alone, without Abby. He didn't want his mother to get any ideas.

* * * *

No wonder he doesn't have a clue about babies. Abby's heart hurt for Blake. Was his, she assumed, ex-wife that much of a bitch to keep the baby away from him, or did Blake stay away?

"Well, while I'm here, you can get in some quality time with Katie."

"As long as I don't feed her broccoli."

The laughter in his voice made Abby smile. "Wasn't your fault. How about you feed her dinner tonight?"

The expression of pure terror on his face caused Abby

42

to burst out laughing. "It won't be horrible, I promise."

Blake shook his head. "The last time didn't work out so well."

"It won't be bad this time. I promise." She picked up her empty plate, glass, and water bottle and carried them into the kitchen. Blake followed. Abby rinsed the plates and put them in the dishwasher, along with the utensils. She reached for the pan on the stove and set it in the sink.

"You're not going to put the pan in the dishwasher?" he asked, placing his mug in the dishwasher.

"No. This is a cast iron pan. You'd ruin it if you put it in the dishwasher."

"Oh."

Abby turned and leaned against the sink. "You really don't know what you have in your kitchen, do you?"

"Umm, no." He glanced over her shoulder. "My sister kind of stocked the kitchen for me."

She glanced at the ceiling and back to him. "Okay, you know where glasses, mugs, plates and utensils are."

"Those are easy."

"I know you know where the garbage can is because it was full of diapers."

"I didn't know what else to do with them." He spread his hands in front of him.

"I know." He was so clueless. In a way it was kind of cute. "Over here." She walked to the other side of the kitchen. "Cabinets below, there is an air fryer, Instant Pot, and Crockpot all in one appliance. Next one has your frying pans, including several cast iron ones. The drawers next to pans have your pots."

"Outside of frying pans and pots, I have no clue what you're talking about." He rubbed his chin.

"It's okay. I can teach you. You'll need to know all of it, if you want to spend more time with Katie. Upper cabinets have your canned foods and pasta." They were pretty bare, though she'd put what she'd ordered in there. "Coffee over here." She tapped the cabinet over the coffee pot.

"I know. I can make coffee."

"I'm sure." She bit her lip so he wouldn't see her grinning. "Toaster in this cabinet. Luckily your sister bought you every type of spoon, spatula, and cooking implement you would need."

"My sister knows I don't cook."

"Do you order out all the time?"

Blake crossed his arms over his chest. "I either eat out or order in. I'm not a cook."

"Well, I can cook while I'm here." She had to go through culinary school to become certified as a pastry chef, but she'd learned how to cook other dishes too.

"I accept." He glanced at her as his watch beeped. "My meeting starts in ten minutes. We can pick up this discussion later."

"Yes, sir." The words slipped from her mouth at his tone.

He inhaled, let his breath out. "Sassy," he murmured before he left the kitchen.

Abby was grateful the counter was behind her to lean on. What was she thinking, saying that to Blake? Maybe it was because he was acting like a CEO instead of a father. She'd really need to watch herself around him. The danger of the innate charm of his derailing her plans was real.

Babbling came from the living room, and she rounded the breakfast counter in time to see Blake disappear into his office.

She and the baby needed to get out of the apartment

for a while, but she needed a stroller. She doubted Blake had one. She picked up the phone and called downstairs. "Hi, Walter. It's Abby. By any chance do you know if there is a stroller I could borrow?" She could rent one, but she'd only do it as a last resort.

"Yes, Miss Abby. We actually have one in the lost and found unclaimed. Shall I bring it up to you."

"That would be wonderful, thank you." She hung up and looked at Katie. "You and I are going to get some fresh air."

Some very much needed air. And distance.

Chapter 4

Blake pushed back from his desk and stood. So much for simple calls. His first call had blown up, and no one had their reports ready on the second one. He rubbed the back of his neck before stretching.

Halfway through the first call, the idea of adding scotch to his coffee was sounding better and better. His team had hashed out the problem, and he'd let them run with it, even if he wanted to jump into the middle with a possible solution. He'd hired the best people, and it was better to let them do their jobs. They'd worked out a solution—eventually—but it had taken longer than he expected.

Grabbing the coffee mug off his desk, he made his way out of his office. Total silence greeted him. Where was Katie? Abby? The play pen was empty, and Abby's bedroom door was open. "Abby?"

Nothing. His gut clenched. Where were they? Pulling out his cell, he scrolled through his contacts. She wasn't there. Of course not. He hadn't bothered to get her cell number because he never expected her to leave the apartment.

Now what? Call the police? And say what? *Sorry to bother you, but my nanny has disappeared with my niece.* Yeah, he could see the headlines in the Seattle papers: *Blake Ellington Calls Police Over Missing Baby and Nanny. Whose baby is it?* That was the last thing he needed.

The door clicked, and he turned. Abby, pushing Katie in a stroller, came waltzing into the apartment.

"Hi," Abby said with a smile. "Done with your meetings?"

"Where have you been?" His voice was rough.

Abby's smile faded. "We went for a walk." She bent over and took Katie out of the stroller. "I left you a note."

Blake looked to where she pointed. He picked up the piece of paper. *Blake, it's a nice day, and Walter found a stroller for Katie. We're going for a walk, be back soon. Abby.* He closed his eyes. He hadn't thought to look for a note. His only thought had been what might have happened to Katie and Abby.

"Sorry, I didn't see it, and the apartment was empty when I came out of my office. I…panicked." Katie cooed and held her arms out to Blake. He froze.

"She wants you to hold her." Abby stepped closer. "Here." She took the mug from his hand as she placed Katie in his arms.

He stopped breathing, afraid she'd start to cry again. Katie grinned up at him, and he relaxed. "Hi, sweetie," he said softly, amazed how she smelled of baby and sunshine. Fresh and clean. Plus, she was smiling at him, not screaming her head off.

Katie patted his chin and babbled at him as Abby went into the kitchen. "Where did you get the stroller?" he asked.

"Walter had one in lost and found. He cleaned it up and brought it up to me."

"Who's Walter?" He propped his hip against the door jamb while holding Katie, who now pounded on his shoulder.

"Your concierge." She shook her head. "Blake, I'm sure you know who he is."

"Maybe." He tried to recall the man but couldn't.

Abby shook her head. "You might run a billion dollar company, but you don't pay attention when you need to."

"What do you mean?" He was curious, but also intrigued.

"I mean"—she opened the fridge—"you don't know who Walter is; you barely know Katie, but I bet you could tell me everything about your company."

"Of course I could. That's my job."

Abby turned to him, exasperation etched on her features. "Let me ask you this: Do you know anything about any of your employees?"

Where was this coming from? Blake stared at her, and Katie began wiggling when she saw the food Abby had begun to heat up. "Easy, young lady." He tightened his hold on the baby.

"Put her in her high chair, and give her some of these." Abby held out a box of banana cookies. Blake took the box and carried Katie into the dining area. He set the box on the table, and stared at the high chair. How hard could this be?

* * * *

Abby bit her lip as Blake tried to figure out the high

chair. How was this man ever going to survive being on his own with this child? Probably not until she was a teenager, and there would be another set of issues.

She warmed up food for Katie and took it out while she fought against laughing. There were cookies everywhere. "Don't!" she yelled when Blake picked up the box to give Katie more.

"You said give her cookies."

"I said give her some, not the entire box." She shook her head. "She's not eating them. She's throwing them on the floor."

"Better than screaming."

Abby could only stare at him. "Here." She placed the sectioned baby plate in front of him with a baby spoon. "Chicken and rice, carrots, and apple sauce." Abby pointed to each section.

"You want me to feed her?"

"Yes. The more you're with Katie, the more she'll bond with you."

"I'm not sure I'm qualified."

Katie threw another cookie, this time at Blake.

"None of that, young lady." Abby scooped the rest of

the cookies off the tray. Katie opened her mouth, and Abby tapped her on the nose so she laughed instead. "Put a little of the chicken and rice on the spoon and put it into her mouth."

Abby watched Blake do as she'd instructed. Katie was hungry, so as the spoon got close, she opened her mouth, and closed it around the food.

"Pull the spoon out."

"It won't hurt her?"

"No." Abby watched as Blake continued to feed Katie. "You're doing fine. Is a chicken Caesar salad okay for lunch?"

"It's fine." His attention was steady on the spoon from bowl into Katie's mouth, the concentration in his features adorable in her eyes. Abby marveled how clueless he was, but he seemed awestruck each time he successfully fed Katie. His willingness to try made Abby's heart sing.

She quickly made salads for both of them, and when she returned to the dining area, Blake was sitting there with applesauce on his shirt. "Oh no, what happened?"

"Someone spit her food at me." His forehead wrinkled as he frowned.

"Well, either she doesn't like it or she's done. Try again."

Blake took a deep breath and tried again. This time Katie turned her head away. "So what does that mean?"

"She's probably full." She glanced at the plate. Everything else was gone but the applesauce. "It's okay." She grabbed the wipes off the counter and handed him one. "Time to wipe her face and hands."

"Didn't I hire you to do this?"

Abby stiffened. The man was very good at reminding her she was the hired help. She needed to remember that. "You did."

He gave her a confused look, but she ignored him as she cleaned Katie up, released her from the high chair and put her in the playpen. Within a minute, Katie was falling asleep. Ignoring Blake, Abby took the baby plate into the kitchen and washed it.

"I've got another call coming up. I'm going to change, and I'll eat in my office," Blake commented.

"Okay." She watched him pick up his salad and disappear into his bedroom. Maybe having him feed Katie hadn't been such a good idea, but the man really did need to bond with his daughter.

Sitting down at the table, she ate her salad and tried to think of ways to get Blake to be with Katie. She'd done this with several families, but it didn't always work. In this case, she had a feeling there was something holding Blake back.

But it was more than that. The man didn't seem to notice people. Like they were gnats to be ignored, especially employees. He never answered her question about knowing anyone in his company. Admittedly, Katie had chosen that moment to make her presence known, but still, he should be able to name his inner circle without thinking. It seemed to her Blake was isolating himself. Not a good thing.

She had to be honest with herself, Blake wasn't part of her job. She'd always take a more holistic approach to being a nanny, though. The whole family needed to be happy, and she wanted to see him relax a little more. Abby sighed. Her place was to take care of Katie as Blake had reminded her.

* * * *

Blake sat at his desk staring at the screen. Why had he

gotten so upset with Abby? Feeding Katie had gone well until the applesauce, but it wasn't Abby's fault. All her questioning had gotten to him.

Of course, he knew his employees. He placed a call to his CFO, and within a minute, Jeff was on camera with him.

"What's up, Blake?"

"Are you still dating the model?" Surprise crossed Jeff's face caused Blake to pause.

"No. That was six months ago."

Blake didn't know what to say. Could Abby be right?

"What's going on, Blake? You're not one to call with idle chit-chat."

He wasn't. "It's nothing. Just an unwanted memory. Talk to you later." Blake ended the call and sat back in his chair.

His job was to make the company money and to provide his employees with stable jobs. He didn't need to know everything about them. Including Abby. She was good at being a nanny, and it was all he needed to know.

With that settled in his mind, he went back to work. If he worked flat out for the rest of the afternoon, he could get the new proposal together.

* * * *

Abby put the finishing touches on dinner. She'd opted for something simple tonight instead of what she'd planned yesterday: spaghetti with meatballs and garlic bread. Katie could eat cut up spaghetti and mashed meatballs without sauce. Early this morning, Abby had put the sauce and meatballs in the crockpot to simmer all day.

When she lifted the lid, it smelled heavenly. It was her own recipe for the sauce, one she had fun with in culinary school. She drained the spaghetti and poured it into a bowl. The sauce and meatballs were already in another.

She carried everything to the table she'd set earlier. She hadn't seen or heard from Blake since lunch. It was almost six. Surely he was done working for the day. Going over to his office door, she knocked softly.

"Come in."

He didn't sound happy. Taking a deep breath, she pushed the door open and poked her head in. "I just wanted to let you know dinner is ready."

"What?" His head swiveled. "It's almost six?"

"Yes, it is."

"Thank you for interrupting me. I'll be right there."

Abby nodded and backed out of the room. Blake's hair was mussed, much like the first time she saw him. She had to wonder if work was frustrating him. After stopping in the kitchen to get the garlic bread for the table, Abby picked Katie up and put her in the high chair.

Katie had been curiously quiet this afternoon. Had she picked up on the tension between Abby and Blake? Abby hoped not. She didn't want to upset the baby any more than she'd already been upset. She cut up some of the pasta and mashed a bit of a meatball and placed it on the tray.

Katie gibbered as she picked the food up in her fist and shoved it into her mouth. Her little eyes went wide, and she grabbed more. At least she liked it. Abby grinned.

"Dinner smells good," Blake remarked as he walked to the table.

"Something simple." Abby was cutting up more pasta for Katie.

"Someone's enjoying herself."

"I think she likes it." Abby kept her gaze on Katie or her food.

"I smell garlic and cheese," Blake commented.

"Cheesy garlic bread in the basket. I didn't use a lot of garlic since I wasn't sure if you liked it." Abby took a bite of her food.

"I do." He took a bite of the bread and groaned. "I'm going to need to run a couple of extra miles on the treadmill."

"I don't see why." Abby closed her eyes. How could she let something like that slip out? The room was silent, so Abby opened her eyes to see Blake staring at her. Those hazel eyes regarded her with interest.

Katie banging on her tray brought Abby out of her trance. "Yes, Katie." She placed more cut up food on Katie's tray.

Blake cleared his throat. "I'm sorry for the way I acted earlier."

She waved aside his apology. "It's nothing."

"It's not. While I did hire you to take care of Katie, you're right. I do need to bond with her a little bit. I might not see her often, but I do want her to know who I am."

It was on the tip of Abby's tongue to ask him why he didn't see his daughter, but it wasn't any of her business. "Just spend some time with her."

"I will." His firm tone left Abby no doubt he would try. "Do you enjoy being a nanny?"

"I like it." She did, but soon she would give it up for her dream of being a pastry chef. She hoped she could make a go of it. Her sister was in her last year in college and would have her degree soon, so expenses would be down, giving Abby the time to get on her feet with her own career.

"You're very good with Katie."

"She's a good baby. You just had a bad night with her."

"Things were a little crazy." He continued to eat. "This is really good. Better than my favorite Italian restaurant, and I didn't think it could happen."

"Thank you. I like cooking." As an adult, she did, but as a teenager, she'd hated it. Maybe because her mother critiqued every little thing Abby did. When her mother was home.

"Your cooking talents are being wasted. I bet most of the families you work for don't appreciate your food."

"I don't cook for all the families I work for. It's rare for me to take a 24/7 job anymore. Usually I do after school things with the kids until their parents get home, I leave."

"So you've been a nanny a long time?"

Abby wondered at Blake's questions, but they were nothing she hadn't answered before with other families. "Eight years." It had taken her a while to build up to her current skill level. Her brother was three years younger than she was and her sister, four. It hadn't been easy going to college and making sure they were taken care of, but she'd done it.

"You're frowning. Should I not be asking you these questions?"

"It's fine." Abby forced herself to relax. Blake wasn't being invasive with his question. "I have a question or two for you."

"Go for it."

"How did you decide on your line of work?"

He tilted his head as he studied her. "Do you know what I do?"

"You're the owner of a large corporation, but I don't know what you do." The articles she'd read hadn't revealed much.

"I run Ellington International, and yes, we are a large

corporation. Basically, I work with companies that are in trouble."

"Financial?"

"Sometimes. Sometimes it's personnel or the manufacturing process."

"So you go in and fix them?" She was curious. She knew he'd been in meetings most of the day.

"In a way. Are you sure you want to hear this?"

"I do." She checked on Katie, who was happily eating spaghetti.

"Basically, I buy the company, restructure them, and get them turning a profit."

Abby frowned. "You destroy an existing company." She'd seen it enough over the years; it was one of the reasons she wanted to work for a family-owned restaurant and not a chain.

Blake shook his head. "Don't judge me by what others do." He pushed away his empty plate. "I rarely lay anyone off. I look at the structure of the company and work with them to improve their situation. My goal is to get them up and running to their full potential."

"I'm sorry." The words flowed out of habit from her

lips even though she'd promised herself she'd stop apologizing over things. She'd done enough of it when she was younger.

"No need." He held up his hand when she opened her mouth. "I don't talk to the public about what I do because no one would believe me."

"That's unfair."

"It is. Most see companies like mine as the enemy, but I enjoy helping a company thrive."

Katie let out a yell, and Abby's attention was drawn to her. "I think you're done." Grabbing a wipe from the pack she'd put on the table earlier, she cleaned the baby up and placed her on the floor. Luckily, she hadn't thrown her food on the floor this time, so there was minimal clean-up.

"Katie's crawling. Why don't you keep an eye on her while I clear the table?"

When she returned from the kitchen, Blake was sitting on the floor with Katie. They were staring at each other with confused expressions. Abby walked over to the playpen and pulled out a couple of toys. "Entertain her." She dropped the toys in Blake's lap and went back to clearing the table.

From the open kitchen, she could see Blake pick up the teddy bear and wiggle it in front of Katie, who squealed and reached for the bear. Abby smiled and turned her attention back to her work.

When she emerged from the kitchen twenty minutes later, Blake was quietly talking to Katie, who was enraptured by him. *You're not the only one.* No matter how hard she tried, Blake fascinated her.

Nope. She didn't need to go there. He was a client, and she didn't mess with clients. Under any circumstances. Abby tiptoed into her bedroom to get everything ready for Katie's bedtime.

* * * *

Out of the corner of his eye, Blake saw Abby make her way into her bedroom. He'd been very aware of her doing dishes. Why was he so attracted to her? Yes, she was a beautiful woman, but it was more than looks.

She had a kind and gentle heart. He'd seen the way she took care of Katie, in the way she reacted when he talked about his job, heck even in the way she took care of him by making meals.

He had to admit, his apartment was clean. He'd

canceled his housekeeper for this week because of Katie and figured he'd have to pay the housekeeper double, but Abby was keeping everything picked up and clean.

He'd never known a woman like her. Of course, he wouldn't. When he did date, it was either some model or an heiress with her own money. He'd found the only way to share the company of women and preserve his own sanity was to stay in his lane. Did Abby care about his money? Would she have taken the job if he hadn't agreed to pay four times the going rate?

Katie laughed, and Blake returned his attention to her. His niece was adorable. Abby was right; he needed to spend time with Katie. He'd talk with his sister when she came back and see if maybe he could give her a break now and then.

His mother was right. His sister and her husband hadn't had time alone since before Katie was born. He couldn't imagine how crazy that was. *You're starting to care.* The thought passed through his head.

It wasn't he didn't care. Growing up, he'd been responsible for his family. His father had left shortly after Rebecca was born. His mother worked two jobs to keep a roof over their heads and food on the table. He did odd jobs around the neighborhood. When he turned thirteen, he also took on delivering newspapers. He worked hard, making sure his sister and mother were taken care of to the best of his ability. Eventually, those odd jobs helped pay his way through school and build his empire. His family wasn't poor anymore because of him. He felt good about it.

Abby walked back into the room, and his attention was captured by her once again. There were times he saw moments of sadness cross her features, and he wondered why. This was one of those times.

The teddy bear Katie held landed in his lap, and he laughed. "Are you trying to get my attention?" He ran his fingers over her belly, and she laughed.

"Would you like to give Katie her bath tonight?" He noticed she had two towels in her hand.

Blake held his hands up. "I don't think I'm ready."

"Okay. I'll go get the water ready."

"Why the kitchen?" He rose from the floor, and picked Katie up.

"You don't have a bathtub, and the bathroom sink is too small."

"Oh, I never thought about it." He hadn't. The showers had been part of the upgrade on the apartment, and since he never expected to have a child here, a tub didn't make sense.

"The sink works until she gets bigger." Abby turned on the water, set the towels on the counter and began pulling things out of the cabinet.

"What is all that?" he asked. It seemed like so much for a baby's bath.

"Baby shampoo, baby body wash, and lotion."

She put her hand under the running water, made an adjustment, and put the stopper in place. "How did you do that?" he asked, gesturing to the sink now filling with water.

"You align the strainer/stopper." She stared at him. "Have you never done it?"

"Every time I try it the water continues to drain." He shrugged his shoulders. Katie cooed and reached out to Abby. "I think someone knows it's her bath time."

"She does." Abby expertly took Katie and laid her on one of the towels on the counter.

"May I stay and watch?" He was curious, mainly

because, until now, he'd never known how much work went into taking care of a baby.

"Sure."

Blake stood off to the side as Abby undressed Katie, cooing and talking to her the entire time. Abby shut off the water and put her fingers in the water once again before lowering Katie into the sink.

"You tested the water again, to make sure it's not hot, right?"

"Yes. You want to bathe the baby in warm water. Her skin is more sensitive than ours, so you don't want it overly hot."

"Oh." Another thing he didn't know. Why would he?

He kept his gaze on Katie as Abby bathed her. She cleaned her body and washed what hair Katie had. When she was done, she lifted Katie out of the water onto the towel and wrapped her up.

"Usually I'd have a special baby towel, one with a little hood on it, but since I don't have one, I make do." She ran a washcloth over the baby's head.

"Why don't you buy one?"

"No sense in it for just one week. I'm sure her mother

has plenty of them, and I can do without."

Blake frowned. "It was okay to buy anything you needed."

"You made that clear." She expertly dried off a wiggling Katie, put a diaper on her, and put her pajamas on. "I didn't see it as a necessity." Abby handed him Katie. "Why don't you take her in and lay her down in the crib, and I'll be right there."

He wasn't sure he was ready for this, but Katie snuggled against his shoulder with a yawn. Poor thing was tired. Once inside the guest bedroom, he paused at the crib. How did one lay a baby down?

Were you supposed to put them on their backs? Or stomachs? Were babies side sleepers? So much he didn't know. Abby walked into the room.

"How do I put her down?" he asked.

"On her back."

"I thought babies slept on their stomach?"

"On their back is better for the first year."

Blake laid Katie on her back. She cooed and kicked her legs. "Do I cover her?"

Abby glanced at him. "You can try. She'll probably

kick the blanket off."

He picked up the small blanket and placed it over her. Katie stopped moving and stared at him, unsure what was going on. She screwed up her face and let out a wail.

"What did I do?" Blake stepped back with his hands up.

"Nothing. Shhh, Katie." At the sound of Abby's voice, Katie stopped crying. "All you need to do is talk to her."

"I think I've done enough." He turned and left the room. A few minutes later, Abby came out of the bedroom. "You make it look so easy."

"It will be once you get the hang of it."

"The baby monitor?" he asked.

"On the counter." She pointed to the white box. "I leave it there because the only other time I need it is when I'm in the shower."

An image of a nude Abby rushed into his head, and his dick grew hard. It was the last thing he needed right now. He thought about going into his office but changed his mind.

"Would you like to watch TV?"

"I have my book." She picked up her tablet from the table. "But don't let that stop you."

He nodded and flipped his big screen TV on. He found an old disaster film he liked, put it on, and slowly relaxed against the sofa. Abby kicked off her shoes, curled up in one of the plush armchairs, and opened her tablet.

Blake tried to ignore how cute she looked with her legs curled under her, holding her tablet and reading. Most women he'd dated were chatter boxes. They were rarely quiet, even when they watched a movie. After a few minutes, he noticed how peaceful the apartment was. It was more than Katie not crying. Even with the quiet drone of the TV, there was something comforting, even companionable, in the silence between them. For the first time, he was truly relaxed around a woman.

* * * *

Abby fought to keep her breathing even as she re-read a paragraph for the fifth time. Her concentration had disappeared. Blake was the problem, sitting there relaxed, watching a movie, and half asleep. The man had gotten under her skin. She was having trouble ignoring him.

Why? She'd been around handsome men before. His

wealthy status should have put her emotions under lock and key. But no. Even now, as he lounged on the sofa, totally at ease, she wanted to go over to him and curl up in his lap.

Her fingers tightened around her tablet. Not a good idea. *You're here to do a job not jump the dad.* Oh but her body so much wanted to be close to Blake. Ugh. She needed to get her thoughts and body under control.

The TV screen flashed, and she glanced up. "You like disaster films?" she asked.

"Yeah. A guilty pleasure."

"They are." She didn't have a lot of time for TV, but there were nights where she couldn't sleep, and she'd try to find a disaster film on.

"You like them too?" Surprise crossed his face.

"Yep." Abby closed her tablet. She wasn't reading anyway. They watched in compatible silence until a commercial came on. Abby stood and stretched and checked on Katie. "She's still sleeping."

"Good. Why don't you sit on the sofa with me to watch the rest of the movie?"

Abby considered his offer. While the chair was

comfortable, she had to turn her head to watch the TV. "Okay." She walked over and sat at the other end of the sofa.

The buttery material curved to her body, and she sighed.

"Tired?" Blake asked.

"No. Oh, I just remembered…" She jumped up. Just as the commercial ended, she walked into the room with two plates. "I made dessert today." She handed him a plate, fork, and napkin.

"What are these?"

"Mini pies." If she said the actual name of the dessert he wouldn't know what it was. "Pastry shells filled with chocolate, caramel, and banana slices, topped with whipped cream."

Blake used his fork and took a bite. His eyes widened. "This is delicious."

Abby's pride swelled. She'd learned how to do some simple but fancy desserts on her own. This one was one of her favorites. She took a bite of her dessert, enjoying the sweetness.

The movie came back on, and they ate and watched in

silence. At the next commercial, Blake stood, took her plate and carried it into the kitchen. Abby leaned her head against the sofa and closed her eyes. She'd rest for a minute.

* * * *

Blake rinsed the plates and left them in the sink. Abby's cooking talents were being wasted. He wondered if she ever thought about changing careers. Her eyes were closed when he returned to the family room.

A squeal came from the baby monitor. He didn't want Abby to jump up, so he went in to check on Katie.

"What's up, sweetie?" Katie eyes were wide open, her arms and legs waving. Blake reached down and picked her up. "Oh…I know that smell." For a half second Blake thought about waking Abby, but decided against it. He could change a diaper. He'd done it before she arrived.

He grabbed a diaper and the wipes and carried Katie into the bathroom. After placing a towel on the counter, he laid the cooing baby down. Couldn't be horrible, right? Quickly, he undressed her and opened her diaper.

"You are a stinky little thing." Luckily, it was nothing like he'd experienced the other night. With one wipe he had her all cleaned up, rediapered, and dressed. When he went to lay her back down, Katie scrunched up her face. "Oh, sweetie…" He picked her up. He really didn't want to wake Abby.

He carried Katie out to the living room. Abby's eyes were still closed. Good. She'd been working hard and deserved a little down time. Sitting down, he cradled Katie against his chest and watched the movie.

Katie snuggled against him, and something inside him loosened. She really was a good baby. But he didn't want to be responsible for her 24/7, but for this short period of time, why not? His sister deserved a break, and his mother needed to heal.

* * * *

Blake woke with a start. He blinked. Katie shifted on his chest, and he glanced down to find her sound asleep. Turning his head, he saw Abby blinking awake.

"Oh goodness," she whispered. "I didn't mean to fall asleep." Her blue eyes were soft and drowsy.

"It's fine," Blake said, shifting slightly. "I'll go put her in her crib." He maneuvered to his feet and carried Katie into the bedroom. He returned a moment later to see

Abby standing up and stretching. Her breasts strained against the t-shirt she was wearing, and his mouth watered.

"You should have woken me."

"Why? Katie just needed a diaper change. I took care of it. But she didn't want to go back into her crib. I think I did fine."

"I didn't mean that. You did great. But it is my job."

"Maybe." He couldn't help staring at her. "You need some down time too."

"You hired me for 24/7."

He shook his head. "Why are we arguing about this?"

Abby huffed. "I have no idea." She rubbed her eyes.

Blake had an idea, though he wasn't so certain it was a good one. He stepped close to her and placed his hands on her shoulders. Abby jumped but didn't pull away. "You're beautiful," he whispered.

"Blake."

"I want to kiss you." He was making his intentions clear before he dropped his head and pressed his lips against hers.

Warm breath whispered against his skin as she leaned into him. He parted his lips, and his tongue stroked along the seam of her mouth. When she opened her mouth, he could taste the chocolate and caramel from earlier.

He slipped his hands from her shoulders to her waist, cradling her close. In turn, her arms encircled his neck. Part of his brain warned him this wasn't a good idea, but the other part encouraged him to continue. Abby wasn't pulling away.

Soft curves against his body caused his blood to heat as they continued to kiss. It had been a while since he'd felt this kind of attraction to a woman. Not the scratch-an-itch attraction, but a deep appreciation for who she was.

He released her lips, and their quick breaths filled the air. He gazed down at Abby. Her cheeks were pink, her eyes wide, and her lips swollen.

"This isn't a good idea," she whispered.

"Why not? We're both consenting adults." It didn't matter he'd just been thinking the same thing. He liked having her in his arms.

"I work for you."

"Technically, you work for Practically Perfect Nannies. I hired them."

Abby titled her head, causing her ponytail to swing to

one side. "True, but…" She shook her head and pulled herself from his hold. "I'm sorry." She scooted around him and into her bedroom.

What the heck just happened? Blake thought about going to her door and knocking, but he didn't want to wake Katie. Blowing out a breath, he shut off the TV and lights and made his way into his bedroom, confused.

Tomorrow, he and Abby were going to have a talk. One kiss and he was lost in her, and he wanted to follow the attraction wherever it led. There was a reason she'd run just now, and he was damned sure going to find out what it was. He wanted more of Abby Thomas. Much more. But it had to be willingly.

Chapter 5

Abby leaned against the bedroom door, trying to calm her racing heart. What the heck had she just done? She kissed Blake. Heat filled her body. She pushed herself away from the door and rubbed her forehead.

"That was a stupid thing to do, Abby," she whispered to herself. She tried to blame being half asleep, but it would be a lie. Abby tried never to lie to herself. When Blake put his hands on her shoulders, a shaft of excitement shot through her veins. When he lowered his head...

She groaned and shook her head. Kissing him wasn't part of the plan. He was Katie's father. Inside her bathroom, she put her pajamas on and splashed her still flaming face with water. How was she going to face him tomorrow?

Be professional. That was the key. Her heart tightened in her chest, and she closed her eyes. It had to be this way. Blake was a rich playboy. She was nothing but a momentary distraction. He wasn't interested in her for anything more than a fling.

Abby needed to remember herself she wasn't the fling type. She wasn't like her mother and would never be, no matter how tempted she was by Blake. Determination stiffened her back and lifted her head. She was here to do her job, and that was it.

Marching out of the bathroom, Abby checked on Katie, who slept peacefully, before she climbed into bed, tossing and turning in a futile effort to find a comfortable spot. Her body was still on fire, and her mind and heart wouldn't let the kiss go. Sleep was going to be a long time coming tonight.

* * * *

Abby glanced at the clock. It was after ten, and she hadn't seen Blake. It shouldn't bother her, but it did. Should she check on him? She took a step toward his closed office door, and stopped.

No. He was able to take care of himself. Besides the coffee pot had been on when she got up this morning. He'd probably gotten up early and gone right to work. She'd give him until eleven, before she'd leave a note.

He'd been really upset yesterday when she left

without telling him, but she wasn't going to wait for him to show his head. It was a beautiful day, and it was good for her and Katie to get out of the apartment for a while. She'd found a nearby park on her map app and wanted to explore it with Katie.

While Katie played in her playpen, Abby inventoried the food. They were doing pretty well, but would need a few items. She made a quick list on her phone. Maybe she'd pick them up while she was out. She'd seen a small local grocery store on her walk yesterday.

As she walked back into the living room, Blake opened his office door. Abby stopped in her tracks. Until this moment, every time Abby had encountered Blake, he was wearing tailored pants and a white shirt, and a couple of times a suit jacket and tie. Not today. Oh, and there was one time when he came in from working out, but she'd forced herself not to stare at him.

Today, he was dressed in jeans and a University of Washington t-shirt. It looked as if he hadn't shaved this morning—he had a slight scruff—and his hair…messy; it made her want to run her fingers through it. She swallowed. Both clung to his body. He was holding a coffee mug and a plate.

"Good morning." She tore her gaze from him to where Katie was in her playpen.

"Morning. I was up, so I got an early start to my day. I had some toast and coffee. Was the coffee still hot when you got up?"

"Yes, thank you."

"Good." He carried the mug and plate into the kitchen, and Abby fought not to stare at his ass. Damn, what was it with men and their tight asses.

Katie giggled and held her arms up, and Abby picked her up. Finding one of the sweaters she bought, she slipped it on Katie.

"Looks like I came out just in time. Taking Katie out for a walk?"

"Yes, it's a nice day."

"Good. Do you mind if I go with you?"

Abby jerked her head up and stared at him. "You want to come with us?"

"Yes. I've been thinking about what you said, I need to bond with Katie. So for the next few days, I'm only working in the morning for a few hours and the rest of the day is for the two of you."

Abby's breath caught in her throat. He was going to spend time with her and Katie. Time with Katie was a good idea, but with her? Nope. "Okay." No, no, no. Her libido had answered before her brain could stop it.

She placed Katie in the stroller and fastened her in. When she straightened, Blake was right there. Her heart pounded. His aftershave teased her nose. A woodsy scent of some sort.

"May I?" He gestured to the handles of the stroller.

"Sure." Abby watched him wheel the stroller around, open the door, and she followed them out and locked the door. The ride down in the elevator was quiet. In the enclosed space, she got another whiff of his aftershave. Sandalwood and rose. She closed her eyes and swayed toward Blake. Nope. She forced herself to straighten. Once outside, she took a deep breath. This was better, other scents to clear out her head.

"Where to?" His deep voice brought her out of her musings.

"Right. There's a park several blocks over, plus a local store I want to stop in."

"Your wish is my command." He turned the stroller, and they started walking. "Katie, it's a very nice day here in Seattle. You need to learn to enjoy them when it's like this because rain is always around the corner."

Abby's lips turned up, and Blake gave a running commentary as they walked. It was cute, but it was more. His voice was deep and soothing. Katie would coo and make noises as if she was answering Blake at times.

This was good. Father and daughter needed to bond. They arrived at the park, and Abby led him over to the baby swing.

"Is it safe?" he asked.

"Yes. As long as you're careful." She gestured to Katie. "Go ahead and take her out and place her in the swing."

"Me?" For a second, something akin to fear passed over his features. "All right." It took him a minute to figure out the stroller fastenings, but he managed to get Katie out and settled in the swing.

Katie pounded the swing and giggled.

"What now?" Blake looked at her.

"Did you put the safety strap around her?"

"Safety strap?"

Abby unclipped it from the diaper bag handle. "This." She handed him the fabric strap. "Put it around the back of the swing, then fasten her in the swing.

Blake took it from her and studied it for a moment before he tried to put it around Katie. "Katie, sweetie, hold still."

Abby fought not to laugh as Katie wiggled in the swing and swung her arms, but he finally got it fastened. "Okay, done."

"Good job. Now give her a push."

Blake nudged the swing, it barely moved.

Abby laughed. "Let me show you." She moved him to the side and gave the swing a push.

Katie let out a big laugh.

"Are you sure she won't fall out?"

"That's why we used the safety strap, and it's not like you're going to push her hard and high. Just little pushes to make her laugh."

He shook his head but gave her a bigger push this time. Katie laughed, her arms and legs moving. "She likes it."

"Yes, she does." Abby watched the enjoyment on Blake's face. He was very intent on Katie and making sure she was safe, but also allowing her to have fun. Poor Katie was going to have an overprotective father as she grew up.

After about ten minutes, Katie stopped laughing and began to fuss. Blake grabbed the swing to a stop. "What it is, Katie?" He looked at Abby.

"She's had enough."

Blake nodded, unclipped Katie, lifted her out, and put her into the stroller. "Pent...Pent." Katie said.

"What does she want?" The confusion on his face was priceless.

"Open the diaper bag, her elephant is inside it."

Blake went to move, and as he did, Katie arched her back. "Shit." Blake caught Katie before she could tumble out of the stroller.

"Kids are wigglers."

"You're telling me." He struggled to fasten Katie into her stroller, but he did it. He retrieved her elephant and handed it to her.

"Pent...Pent..." She waved the small stuffed toy in the air.

"I don't understand how you cope." He brushed his hair back from his forehead.

"You learn." She picked up the swing safety belt and clipped it around the diaper bag handle.

"I guess." He took the stroller by the handle. "Where to now?"

"If you want to walk around the park while I go into the store, I'll be fine." She motioned to the building.

"I'd like to go with you, if you don't mind."

"I don't." They walked in silence to the store and went inside.

Abby loved small local markets. They usually had things items the big chain stores didn't. She grabbed a small carry basket and left Blake to follow her or not. First stop, she picked up a small roast for tomorrow night's dinner, potatoes and carrots. Bananas, peaches, and more dry baby cereal.

Lastly, Abby went down the baking goods isle. She wanted to make a cake. Abby picked out the items she'd need. Her little basket was full. Not unusual. She went looking for Blake and found him near the front of the store staring down at Katie, who had managed to fill her stroller with stuff. Abby burst out laughing, and Blake glared at her.

"I have a little klepto on my hands." There was laughter in his voice.

"She's a baby. She sees something shiny or colorful, and she reaches for it."

"What do I do?"

"Put it back." Abby knelt down. "Miss Katie, you have some odd tastes." She picked the items out of the stroller and handed them to Blake. There weren't many, but Katie's stash was interesting. A small box of baby oatmeal, a packet of gravy, and a set of plastic rings.

"The rings are okay; I gave those to her. I have no clue how she got the rest."

"You probably had her stroller too close to the shelves." She hooked her basket over her arm. "Go put them back, and I'll check out."

"Be right back."

Abby grinned as she pushed Katie up to the checkout. Abby placed the basket on the conveyor belt, and pushed Katie ahead of her. The clerk was over halfway done when Blake showed back up.

"Can I take her outside?" he asked.

"Sure, but first…" Abby reached down and took the plastic keys from the stroller. Katie wailed. "Easy, Katie. We have to pay for them." She held the tag for the clerk to scan, before handed them back to Katie, who went quiet.

"Off we go." Blake took the stroller and left.

"I thought he was going to have a heart attack," the clerk said.

"What?"

"Your husband. When the baby started screaming, he jumped out of his skin and looked panicked."

Abby laughed. "He still isn't used to the baby," she said, but didn't correct the woman about Blake being her husband.

Abby loaded the groceries into her reusable backpack the way she wanted them, paid, and strapped it on. She walked outside to see Blake kneeling and talking to Katie.

"Now, screaming is not the way to get what you want, young lady."

"Are you trying to reason with a ten-month-old?"

"Maybe." He stood. "Where's the groceries?"

"Right here." She turned and pointed to her back.

"I should carry those for you." He held his hand out.

"I'm fine."

"So what's on the agenda when we get back?" Blake asked.

Abby couldn't help but grin. "No agenda really. Katie will probably want a nap. I want to put the steaks in to marinate."

"I'll check the propane in the grill."

"Thank you."

Katie added her voice to the conversation. "You, missy, will be having leftover spaghetti."

More babble.

"Abby's right; you're too little for steak." He glanced at Abby, and she nodded. Blake looked so pleased with himself, Abby had to look away before she kissed him.

Luckily, they turned the corner to the entrance to his building, and Abby tucked her feelings away into a box where they belonged.

Once inside the apartment, Katie started crying. "It's okay, sweetie." Abby dropped the backpack on the counter in the kitchen.

Blake went to unfasten Katie, and she screamed. He

jumped away.

"She's tired." Abby said. "Shhh, sweetie." She quickly unfastened Katie and rubbed her back as she carried her into the bedroom. Abby made noises at Katie while she changed her diaper, and laid her in the crib. She went right to sleep.

"Katie has a set of lungs on her," Blake remarked when Abby returned.

"She does." Abby started to unload the backpack. Blake leaned against the counter by the sink, sipping from a bottle of water.

"You carried all that back." He gestured to the items covering the counter.

"Yes. Why so surprised?" She began putting things away. Dinner tonight would be the steaks, potatoes, and corn.

"I could have carried it."

"You were pushing Katie."

"Yet if I hadn't been there, you would have been pushing Katie and carrying the groceries."

"True, but I'm used to it." She was. While she didn't do shopping for all the families she worked for, occasionally, she'd been asked to pick up staples and more substantial shopping, if she had a vehicle. "It's no big deal."

"It is to me."

Abby turned her head and stared at him. "Blake, I'm more than capable of carrying groceries. They probably weigh a little less than Katie does."

He frowned but didn't say more as she put the groceries away and prepped food and a bottle for when Katie woke up. "Now, what are we going to do?" he asked.

"I'm going to throw a load of Katie's laundry in and check my email. I'm sure you have work to do."

"Remember…" He followed her into the living room. "I'm only working in the morning."

"Oh yeah." Damn, he had said that. She'd counted on him being in his home office to help stave off this impossible attraction she had for him. "Well, do whatever you do when you're home alone. You won't even know I'm here." And she was going to do her darndest to ignore him too. Abby shook her head, finding a million dollars would be easier than trying to ignore Blake Ellington.

* * * *

Blake watched Abby walk out of the kitchen. She acted as if carrying a boat load of groceries was an everyday thing. Maybe for her, but it wasn't for him. He'd been raised to be a gentleman, and it irked him Abby wouldn't allow him to do little things for her.

Abby came out of her bedroom with one armful of clothes and her laptop in another. "Let me help." He reached for the clothes and took them before she could answer.

"Thanks." He carried them to the laundry room and set them down. He glanced at all the buttons on the washing machine. Laundry wasn't something he worried about. His housekeeper took care of it when she was here. Besides, most of his suits went to the dry cleaner.

"Not sure what to do?" Abby commented from behind him.

"Nope." He stepped to the side. The room was small so, when she moved around him, her body brushed up against his. His blood heated.

"Simple, cold water, drop in a detergent pod, add clothes, and hit start." Her actions followed her words, and the machine started. "Simple."

"I guess." He rubbed the back of his neck. Hadn't he done laundry when his mother was working? He didn't remember, but he didn't think so. Dishes, yes. Taking care of his sister, yes, but not laundry.

Abby squeezed by him and out of the room. Blake followed. She sat at the table and opened her laptop. He could go get his and do email, but if he did, one thing would lead to another. He was determined to take some time off, but with Katie sleeping, he was at loose ends.

"How long will Katie be asleep?" This would be a good time for him to go visit his mother.

"About an hour and a half."

Blake glanced at his watch. It was enough time for what he wanted to do. "I'm going to run out for a bit." He grabbed his keys. "I know we just stopped at the store, but do you need me to pick up anything?"

"I'm good. Thanks."

He left the apartment. On the drive to the rehab unit, his mind wondered to Abby. The woman was an enigma to him. Her independence made him want to help her more and more. He suspected Abby was so used to doing things on her own she didn't know how to ask.

Laughter escaped his lips. He should be the one to talk. Didn't he do the same thing in his business? But he was getting better. Now, personal life was different. Maybe tonight, after dinner, he could talk more with Abby. He wanted to know what made her tick.

Blake turned into the parking lot of the rehab unit, parked his car, and checked in at the nurses' station where he was directed to his mother's room.

Maggie was sitting in a chair beside the bed, looking a lot better than the last time he saw her. Gone were the lines of pain, and there was color in her cheeks. "Hi, Mom."

She looked up. Her brown eyes brightened, and she smiled. "Blake, darling. I didn't expect to see you today?"

"I had some free time and thought I'd visit." He snagged the plastic chair and sat. Not exactly comfortable, but the chair and his comfort didn't matter; his mother did.

"Where's Katie?" His mother's forehead wrinkled.

"At my apartment."

"With who? Not that Vanessa woman." His mother sat forward.

"Oh God, no. I hired a nanny from Practically Perfect

Nannies."

"Thank goodness." She relaxed and sat back. "I'd put the card in there for your sister, now I'm glad I did. How is Katie?"

For the next thirty minutes, he filled his mother in on Katie and how she was doing. When the physical therapist came to take his mother off to her appointment, Blake kissed her and told her he would visit again.

"Bring Katie and the nanny next time. I want to see them both." Her eyes gleamed as the nurse wheeled her away.

Blake sat in his vehicle for a few minutes before he drove away. Bring Katie and Abby? He shook his head. A recipe for disaster.

He opened the door to his apartment and heard Katie's laughter. Blake spied Abby on the floor playing with Katie.

"I can feel you staring at me," she said.

"Guilty." Blake walked into the living room.

"Ba, Ba, Ba," Katie babbled crawling over to him.

He looked at Abby.

"I think she's trying to say your name."

Blake grinned, reached down, and lifted Katie into his arms. "Yes, it's Ba, Katie."

Katie laughed and patted his cheek.

Abby stood and brushed off her clothes. He wasn't sure why; she'd vacuumed earlier.

"What did you do while I was gone?" he asked.

"Finished the laundry, folded it, and watched some cooking videos."

"Why cooking videos?"

Abby flashed him a smile. "So I can keep you happy with what I'm feeding you."

Blake laughed. "Seriously?"

She shook her head. "No. I like learning about different ways to prepare food. The videos help me keep my skills up."

"You, Miss…" He shook his finger at her. "…you made me nervous for a moment. Again, you don't have to cook for me."

"True. But I have to eat, and while takeout is nice once in a while, I'd rather have nutritious food."

"The dessert you made last night wasn't nutritious."

She turned in her chair. "Actually, it wasn't bad. The

chocolate and caramel were both sugar-free."

"They were?" He hadn't even noticed. Katie wiggled, and Blake set her in her playpen.

"Yes. Usually, I'll make fruit tarts, which are better for you, but I didn't have the right fruit here."

"What other desserts do you make?"

"I can make all sorts of things, cakes, tortes, pies, cheesecake, cookies, the list can go on and on."

Blake shook his head. "You are so much more than a nanny."

Her cheeks turned pink, and she turned back to her laptop. "I enjoy cooking."

He had a feeling it was more than enjoyment. Blake kept his gaze on her. Abby liked being helpful and feeding people. An idea came to mind. Deciding to act on it, Blake jumped up and strode out of the room.

* * * *

Abby blew out a breath when Blake left the room. She'd managed to dodge his questions about her cooking. It wasn't easy. Why she didn't tell him she was a trained pastry chef she didn't know. Well, maybe she did. When she'd mentioned it before, others would ask why she wasn't doing that job instead of being a nanny.

Very few people understood her commitment to seeing her sister through college and not having major loans for either herself or her sister.

Blake came out of his office with his laptop, sat down on the sofa, and started typing. By the look of concentration on his face, he was busy working on something. Good. Maybe he would ignore her now.

Katie let out a cry, and Blake's head rose.

"It's okay. She just hungry." Abby walked into the kitchen to get a bottle. Blake was still typing away even as Abby sat down to let Katie have her bottle.

"When did she start feeding herself?" Blake asked.

Abby glanced over at him. "She's been holding her bottle since I got here."

"She wouldn't even take it from me the first night, and even when I put the nipple in her mouth, she fussed."

The word nipple coming from Blake's mouth caused her body to heat. Why? It was a normal word. Maybe it was the way he said it in the husky deep voice of his. *Pull yourself together.* "Babies sometimes do that." She kept an eye on Katie as she ate.

"What's on tap for this afternoon?" he asked.

"Some more playtime with Katie, then probably another short nap."

"And what does playtime include?"

Abby glanced at him. "Well, since you want to bond with her. It means you get down on the floor and play with her." *Let's see how that goes over.*

Blake stared at her. His mouth opened and shut. "Is that why you vacuum every morning?"

"You noticed?" Surprised flowed through her veins. She did it during his workout time. It paid to keep the carpet clean with a ten-month old around. They crawled and put everything into their mouths.

"I did. I also notice how you keep the dining room carpet covered with plastic."

"Babies are not tidy eaters. I figured it was better than worrying about the carpet."

"I never noticed this when my mom took care of her."

"Does your mom feed Katie in the kitchen?" Blake nodded. "Easy to clean up there, carpet not so much, especially if she spills something."

"I never thought about it."

"Can I ask how often you've seen Katie since she was born?" She wanted to know more about his relationship with Katie's mother, but wouldn't ask outright.

"A handful of times. Usually at my mom's house."

"Does your mom take care of Katie a lot?" This chat was giving her more information on why he wasn't prepared. It seemed he didn't have a good relationship with the baby's mother.

"Mom helps my sister when she needs it."

"Sister?" Wait a second, did he just say *sister*? Was it possible Katie wasn't his?

"Yeah, my baby sister. Katie is her child."

"You're not the father?" All this time she thought he was a clueless dad, and he wasn't. He's the clueless uncle. It explained so much.

"You thought I was Katie's dad?" The astonishment on his face caused Abby to laugh.

"What was I to think? You called the agency. I get here, and you thrust Katie at me and go to bed. You never mentioned Katie was your niece or you had a sister."

Blake stared at her, and burst out laughing. "Lord, no. I don't need the responsibility of a child in my life."

This didn't surprise Abby. Blake was super focused on his work, or he had been until she told him he needed to bond with Katie. "How did you come to take care of Katie?" Abby almost couldn't believe what she was hearing. But part of her perked up. She didn't have to worry about Katie's momma coming back into Blake's life.

Behave yourself, Abby. Remember you don't do playboys for any reason, even sexy ones like Blake.

"Mom fell and messed up her ankle. My sister and her husband are overseas, and I'm under strict orders not to disturb them. I didn't think taking care of Katie would be a big deal, but I learned quickly I was wrong."

"No big deal? You've never been around an infant. Poor Katie."

"Poor Katie? What about me?"

The astonishment in his voice caused Abby to giggle. "This explains a lot. Was Katie awake or sleeping when you brought her here?"

"Asleep. She slept through the paramedics with my mom, me packing up and getting the baby seat in my car, and all the way into my apartment."

"What did you have her sleeping in?"

"The baby seat thing."

"How long after you arrived here did she wake?" More of a picture was forming.

"About an hour or so. I changed her diaper and warmed a bottle, but she was fussy."

"At least you know how to change a diaper."

"It was a bit of trial and error."

"I bet." Abby rubbed her forehead. "When Katie woke, she didn't understand where she was or who you were."

"But she's seen me before."

"As you said—a handful of times. But she knew your mother, and she wasn't around. No wonder she started crying, and you couldn't get her to stop."

"I almost joined her."

"Poor Blake." Abby reached over and patted his arm.

"Brat." His voice was soft, but she heard him.

"I can be." A laugh sounded from the playpen. "Guess who's done." She scooted around Blake and went into the playpen, telling herself it made no difference Katie wasn't Blake's child. She wasn't going to get involved with him.

She couldn't get involved with him. She had plans, and they didn't include a billionaire playboy who would toss her away on a whim.

* * * *

Blake watched Abby go over to Katie. She'd thought Katie was his? He almost couldn't believe it. As much as Blake didn't want the responsibility of a child, if he had one, he'd step up to the plate and make sure she was taken care of.

Blake wanted to protest but didn't. He watched as Abby took Katie out of the playpen and settled her on the floor, before Abby took several of Katie's toys out of the playpen.

"Keep her entertained," Abby said before she walked into the kitchen.

He closed his laptop and joined the baby on the floor. Katie was sitting and reached for the set of plastic keys.

He shook them before handing them to her. The baby laughed and promptly stuck one in her mouth.

"Does everything go into her mouth?" he asked.

"Yes."

Blake turned his head to see Abby in the kitchen.

"What are you making?"

"Lunch. Nothing fancy. Sandwiches for you and me, and Katie will have some baby food."

"And dinner?"

"Remember, you're grilling the steaks."

A little hand pounding on his leg caused Blake to look at Katie. She was sitting there smiling at him and pounding his leg. He shifted and Katie dropped the keys and rolled to her knees.

Blake froze. "Ah, Abby. Katie is on her hands and knees."

"Is there a problem?"

"Won't she get rug burn?" Abby's laughter floated from the kitchen to him.

"No, she'll pick up her hands and knees as she moves."

"Oh." He watched Katie rock back and forth for a minute, then she was off. "Holy crap."

"What is it?" There was worry in Abby's voice.

"She's fast." Blake watched Katie race to the bedroom door and back, laughing and smiling the entire time.

"She is."

Blake kept his gaze on Katie, who went back to the bedroom, as she started to head back toward him, she veered left. He followed her on his hands and knees. Katie stopped and glanced back at him before laughing and taking off again.

He laughed and followed her saying, "I'm coming to get you."

* * * *

Abby's heart lightened watching Blake chase Katie in the living room. The baby was laughing and so was Blake. For all of his protestations about not wanting a child, he was going to make a great father.

When she'd suggested he get on the floor and play with Katie, she hadn't expect him to do it. And now he was crawling after Katie, who was having the time of her life. For a few minutes, Abby let herself think of them as a family.

Normal routine day, lunch, dad and baby playing. The whole happy family thing. Abby shook her head, dispelling her thoughts. It wasn't in the cards for her, at least not for a while, if ever.

She had her plans. With the pay from this job, she was

one step closer to giving up being a nanny. Laughter pulled her out of her head.

Blake was lying on the floor with Katie pounding on his chest, like a mini-gorilla. Both couldn't stop giggling.

Abby fished her phone out of her pocket and took a couple of pictures. Blake would appreciate them later, and she would be able to look back at this job as a turning point.

"Abba." Katie came racing over toward where Abby stood.

"Easy." Abby stepped out of the kitchen and down the one step to pick Katie up and swing the girl over her head.

"No fair," Blake said from where he lay on the floor.

"Nanny privilege."

"Oh?" His eyes brows rose, but he didn't move from his position.

"BaBa." Katie blathered, and Abby put her down. In an instant, Katie was next to Blake, patting his belly. "BaBa."

"I'm not sure what she's trying to say, but maybe she's hungry." Blake's stomach growled.

"I think you are too." Shivers of awareness slid over

her skin. This was starting to feel too domesticated. "Why don't you put her in her high chair, and I'll be right there with food."

"You got it."

Abby went back into the kitchen before her imagination ran away with her. This was just a job, nothing more, nothing less. That's all it could ever be.

Chapter 6

Blake strode out of his home office Thursday morning, feeling great, having been up and working early, fleshing out his plan. He talked with Jeff, his CFO, who came up with a solid plan for Blake's idea. He wanted to tell Abby about it but needed to wait until Jeff had everything in place.

While they were talking yesterday, he'd done some quick research about the cost of culinary school and found out the average cost and time. Blake wanted to create scholarships for those wanting to attend.

Like all the scholarships his company had created and executed, they were done anonymously. While Jeff and others were always trying to get him to claim credit, Blake refused. He didn't do this because he wanted credit. He did it because he wanted to pay it forward. He'd had help when he went to college, now others would too.

Most didn't understand. Blake wasn't raised with money—not even close. He'd worked his way through high school and college, working and studying. Several scholarships and grants had allowed him to get his degree.

Since he had a head for numbers, he started off in finance. As he progressed, he went after his MBA. Blake worked hard, completing his MBA by age twenty-five. It hadn't been easy. Many thought he wouldn't make it, but he had.

The scent of something doughy brought him out of his musings. "Something smells delicious."

"Good morning," Abby said. "Cinnamon rolls. They're almost ready. Can you check on Katie?"

"Sure." He peeked in the other bedroom, then backed out. "She's still sound asleep."

"I think Uncle Blake wore her out last night."

Blake grinned. "She likes being chased." After dinner, he'd chased Katie all over the apartment. Katie loved every second of it. "Can I come in and get coffee?"

"Of course." Abby had her back to him as she washed fruit. "Did you get everything done at work you wanted?"

"I did, thank you." He took a sip of the hot brew and sighed. "This is so good. Why is it my coffee never taste this good?"

"Because you make it too strong." She set the washed fruit into a big bowl. "I noticed it the other day. You don't need ten scoops for five cups of water."

"How many did you use?"

"Five and five, plus I use a light to medium roast. It really helps with the flavor."

"You're spoiling me."

"How so?" There was confusion in her blue eyes.

"Making me gourmet coffee and your cooking is out of this world."

Her cheeks turned pink, and she looked at her toes. Blake set his mug aside and approached Abby. He lifted her chin up until their gazes met.

"You are special," he whispered.

"I'm really not."

"You are and…" He lowered his head and captured her lips with his. He'd been wanting to do this again.

She placed her hands on his shoulders, and Blake braced himself for rejection, but instead, she slid her fingers behind his head and into his hair. Her body melted against his as her lips parted for him.

In turn, Blake slipped his arms around her waist,

pulling her to him. He wanted this woman. She was more than just a nanny. So much more. When they broke apart, they were both breathing heavy.

"What are we doing?" Abby whispered.

"I would have thought it was obvious." He couldn't keep the humor out of his tone.

"That's not what I meant. You're my employer."

"Technically, the nanny agency is your employer. I hired the agency, not you personally."

"Semantics. We shouldn't be doing this."

"Why not?" He wanted to know what she was thinking.

Abby shook her head.

"No reason then."

"There's a million."

"Give me one."

She opened her mouth, and his cell phone rang. With a curse, he stepped back from Abby and pulled out his phone. "Ellington here."

"Blake, darling, it's Vanessa."

He stiffened. He hadn't talked to Vanessa in months. Glancing at Abby, he motioned he was going to his office.

She nodded, but her movements were stiff.

"Hello, Vanessa," he said once he got behind closed doors. "What can I do for you?"

"Darling, the charity fashion show is next Friday, and you promised to go with me."

"Did I?" He sat down and brought up his calendar. Yep, there it was. He hadn't looked past this week with Katie here.

"Don't make me beg."

"I won't. I forgot about it. Send the details to my phone."

"Of course. Shall we go to dinner before or after the event?"

"Let's decide closer; it depends on how busy I am." He'd make sure he was busy. Just hearing Vanessa's cloying voice made him wish he could go to the event with Abby.

"Very well, darling. Talk to you next week."

The line went dead. Blake took a deep breath. Maybe by the time next week rolled around, he'd have a good excuse to give Vanessa. In fact, the best excuse, he already had a woman in his life. Could he convince Abby to give them a chance?

* * * *

Abby breathed a sigh of relief when Blake closed the door behind him. What the hell was she thinking? She wasn't. That was the problem. The second Blake touched her, all coherent thoughts went out of her head. This was so not good.

The oven timer went off, and Abby pulled the perfectly cooked cinnamon rolls out and set them on the counter. After getting the icing from the fridge, she began frosting the rolls while they were still hot.

Usually, she'd use a piping bag, but she didn't have one, so she used a knife. Not her best decorating job, but it would do. She left several unfrosted. A giggle came over the baby monitor. Katie was awake. Abby set the knife in the sink.

"Good morning, Miss Katie," she said as she walked into the bedroom.

Katie cooed, waving her arms and legs. Abby picked her up, changed her, and dressed her for the day. When they arrived in the dining room, Blake was sitting at the table. Plates had been set out, along with glasses of water and Katie's plastic bowl.

"Good morning, Katie." Blake stood and walked over to them and brushed a kiss over Katie's head. When he looked up, his gaze clashed with Abby's. "Sorry for the interruption."

"No worries." Shaking herself free of his mesmerizing gaze, she placed Katie in her high chair. When she turned, Blake was standing behind her.

Her breath caught in her chest. Why did he affect her like this? Yes, he was sexy, handsome, and oh so male. And she'd worked for handsome men before — but they'd been married or in a relationship. Even if they were single dads, she had no problem ignoring even the slightest attraction. Not with Blake. It was like she was iron filings, and he was a magnet. What was that line from a TV show? Resisting was futile.

"Those rolls look delicious." He held her chair for her. Abby sat down. Another thing she'd noticed about Blake. He was always holding her chair for her, or he'd wait until she sat down before he sat. A gentleman. "I gave us both water, did you want more coffee?"

"Water is good." Abby took one of the unfrosted rolls

and broke it into little pieces before putting it in Katie's bowl and placing the bowl on the high chair tray. Katie grabbed a piece of the roll and shoved it into her mouth.

"I didn't realize babies could eat cinnamon rolls." Blake took two frosted rolls.

"It's okay for them. She's got a couple of teeth."

"She does. I've been bitten."

"When?" Katie didn't seem to be a biter.

"Before you arrived. I was trying to check to see if maybe she was teething, and she clamped down on my finger."

"Ouch." Abby could sympathize as she'd been bitten before.

"Now I know better." He took a bite of the cinnamon roll. The moan left his lips was one of pure pleasure. "Damn, woman. You know how to cook. These melt in my mouth."

Abby couldn't stop the shaft of pride flowing through her at his compliment. "Thank you."

"I mean it. Your talents are wasted."

She shook her head. Being a nanny allowed her to experiment a little more than being in a restaurant environment. She was always very careful to make sure her recipe worked out before she fed it to the families she nannied for.

Katie pounded on the tray, and Abby laughed. "Yes, darling." She put Katie's sippy cup in front of her. In the past few days, Katie's mobility and coordination had improved. Her mother was going to be surprised when she saw her again. "When does your sister get home?"

"Sunday." Blake took two more rolls. He definitely had a healthy appetite, but where did he put it all?

After they finished, Abby cleaned Katie up and put her in the playpen. She started to cry. "What's up, sweetie?"

"I'll take her." Blake lifted Katie out of the playpen.

"You shouldn't pick her up the minute she cries. It isn't good for her."

"Just this once." He winked at her, and Abby's heart pounded. This man disarmed her so easily.

"I'm going to go clean the kitchen and get dinner in the crockpot."

"What's for dinner?" He rubbed his belly with his free hand.

Abby smiled and shook her head. "Roast, potatoes, and carrots."

"Dessert?"

"That's a surprise." She made her way into the kitchen. Abby planned on a special dessert tonight; she'd make it while Katie was down for her afternoon nap.

* * * *

Blake pushed Katie in her stroller as they walked to the park. He was enjoying this time with her and Abby too. Abby was a little quiet after their morning kiss. If his phone hadn't interrupted them, it would have lasted much longer.

It was a nice day for Seattle. Partly cloudy, but not too hot. When they got to the park, Abby let him push Katie in the swing again. He looked at the slide. "Can I put her on the slide?"

"She's too young."

"Okay." While Katie liked swinging, he thought maybe the slide would be something else fun. She was sitting up quite well. "What else can we do with her at the park?"

"We can set her in the play area." Abby pointed to the

area with climbing bars and other things.

"She can't climb yet."

"No, but the wood chips are a good thing for her to play in. They're made for children, and it will be a new texture for her."

Blake hadn't thought of it. When Katie was tired of swinging, he carried her over to the other play area and sat her down. He noticed Abby sat on a bench nearby with the stroller. "Now what?" he asked.

"Sit with her and here"—she tossed him two different plastic balls—"play with her."

Katie patted the wood chips, grabbed one in her hand and started to put it in her mouth. "No, sweetie." Blake took it out of her hand. "Those are not for eating."

Katie giggled.

Blake placed one of the balls in her lap, and Katie pushed it off. He put it back, and she pushed it off again. He grinned. After about fifteen minutes, Katie started to get fussy. He picked her up and turned.

"Over here," Abby called.

He found her and walked toward her. She'd spread a blanket out on the grass and was sitting there with a small basket of things. "When did you pack all this?" He'd noticed she was wearing the backpack again, but thought it was empty.

"While you were getting Katie ready. Nothing big." She spread some of Katie's toys out on the blanket, along with her sippy cup. Katie started bouncing the second Blake set her down. "Just a moment." Abby pulled several baby cookies out of a baggie.

Katie was already reaching for them, her little hands opening and closing. She took one and shoved it in her mouth.

"I never realized how much babies ate," Blake said as he sat down on the blanket. This was nice.

"They eat a lot of small meals." She put her hands in front of her face, took them away and said, "Peek a boo."

Katie started laughing, and Abby did it again. It did his heart good to see the two of them playing. "Your turn," Abby said.

"What?"

"Play peek-a-boo with her."

At first, Blake wasn't sure how he should do it, he shifted and laid on his stomach, elbows on the ground. He covered his face and uncovered it and said, "Boo."

Katie laughed and rocked toward him. He did it again and again. Soon they were all laughing until Katie reared back and fell over. Blake went to jump up, but Abby's arm on his stopped him.

"It's okay," she said softly. "Watch."

Katie lay there for a moment, before she rolled herself over and got to her hands and knees. She crawled over to where Blake was. "Papa."

Blake's mouth fell open.

"Good job, Katie," Abby said.

"But I'm not her dad," Blake said. Something inside him tightened when Katie said "Papa." He tried to shake the feeling away, but it persisted. Maybe she saw another man who made her think of her father. He glanced around the park. Since it was a nice day, there were lots of people with their kids, but mainly women. No dads. Blake wasn't ready to be a dad, probably would never be ready.

"No, but you're the male in her life right now."

"My sister and her husband aren't going to be happy."

"Blake." Abby soft touch had him turning to her. "She's a baby; she's learning new words. She's called me mama a few times."

"Pant. Pant."

Abby laughed. "Yes, elephant." She grabbed the small stuffed animal and handed it to Katie, who cradled it in her lap and yawned. "Someone is getting tired."

"How long have we been out here?" Blake asked, trying to figure out why Katie calling him papa affected him so much. He never planned on having kids. Marrying maybe, but not for several more years.

"A couple of hours." Abby began putting things away. Just as she finished, Katie started crying.

Blake went to put Katie in the stroller, and Katie wasn't having it. She bucked and cried louder. "Katie, sweetie, you need to get in your stroller." But Katie wasn't listening. She threw her elephant on the ground. Blake looked at Abby.

Abby picked up the elephant and put it in her backpack. "Come on, little miss." Abby produced a bottle. "How about you have some juice while we push you home."

Katie reached for the bottle. Abby scooped her up, put her in the stroller, and fastened her in before giving her the bottle. "Watch her as we walk. I suspect she'll be asleep before we get a block or two."

"Okay." Blake started to push the stroller. An older woman was standing at the end of the path. She smiled at them.

"So nice to nice to see young people taking an interesting in their child," the woman said.

"Oh, but…" Abby started.

"Thank you," Blake said and urged Abby to keep walking. When they got to the end of the park, Abby glanced at Blake.

"Why didn't you let me correct her assumption?"

"What harm did her assumption do?" For him, a part of him opened up. Someone besides Abby thought he was doing a good job. While he never needed validation before, this seemed different and so worth it.

"What happens next time you're out with Katie and I'm not here?"

"I doubt I'll see the woman again. No harm no foul." He wondered why Abby was protesting so much? Did she want more? Was it possible he wasn't the only one invested in their kisses? Maybe he'd find out later tonight.

* * * *

Abby put the finishing touches on the mini cakes she'd made before putting them in the fridge. Katie would be up any minute. Her mind wandered back to the park earlier today and the older woman assuming she and Blake were a couple and Katie was theirs.

Why did Abby make a big deal out of Blake not correcting the woman? Abby didn't say anything to the lady at the market the other day. She shook her head. Maybe it was because, at first, Abby was flattered, then reality hit. She couldn't get a man like Blake, nor did she want to. She shook her head. Billionaire playboys weren't for her. Straightening from the fridge, her cell phone rang. Her personal phone, not her nanny phone.

She glanced at the screen. Scrumptious Addiction. "Hey, Paul, what's up?"

"Hi, Abby. I sent you an email, but I know when you're working the nanny job you don't always have time to look."

Abby paused. "Urgent?"

"Sort of. I need you to come to the restaurant on Monday."

"Shouldn't be a problem." The job with Blake was done on Sunday, and her boss promised her next week off.

"Good. Just read the email and get back to me as soon as you can."

"All right." Abby hung up. Paul was being awfully cagey about what the email contained. She cleaned up the kitchen, and opened her laptop with a glance down the hall. Blake's office door was open. She could see him sitting at his desk typing away. A pang of domesticity hit her. Is this what things would be like if they were together?

Abby shook her head. There wasn't going to be anything domestic about her and Blake. Once her email program was open, she located Paul's email and opened it. She read the email four times. He was offering her a full-time job as his pastry chef. *Oh. My. God.* It was all Abby could do to keep herself seated.

This was a dream come true. She'd been working with Paul for over a year now, filling in when he needed extra help, no matter the job. She opened the attachment. It was a contract. Oh, goodness. She put a hand to her chest to keep her heart from jumping right out of her body.

Okay. Breathe, Abby. Breathe and think. She needed

time to read the contract. No jumping without knowing for sure what she was getting into. Abby sent Paul a text saying she got his email, and if it was okay with him, she'd give him her answer on Monday.

Paul texted back it wasn't a problem. If she could arrive at ten on Monday, they could discuss anything she needed. Abby sat back in the chair and closed her eyes. Was it possible her dream was coming true? It was hard for her to believe after all these years.

* * * *

"You're very quiet tonight," Blake said after they put Katie to bed. It wasn't like Abby was a chatter box, but she seemed subdued.

"I'm sorry. I'm a little distracted."

"That's okay. Do you need to talk about the distraction?"

"It's fine." She gave him a quick smile and deflected. "I have a special dessert for you tonight."

Blake watched her rise and go into the kitchen. She returned a few minutes later with two plates, forks, and napkins. He took one of the plates from her and looked at the cake. He dipped his finger in the frosting. "Chocolate

125

whipped cream?" he asked.

"Yes. Is it too sweet?"

"It's perfect." He cut a piece of cake with his fork and put it into his mouth. "I keep saying this, but dang it, it's true. Your talents are wasted."

"Thank you. Does it taste okay?"

"Why so worried?" The cake was light, fluffy, and moist. The best he'd ever tasted.

"I tried something new. I was pretty sure it was going to work."

"So I'm a guinea pig?" He smiled at her.

"Sort of." Her lips twitched. "I tasted it as I mixed it up."

"Tell me what's in it." This woman was a genius in the kitchen. The roast tonight had been perfect, along with the potatoes and carrots. And the gravy. Blake thought he'd died and gone to heaven. He was going to miss her cooking. Well, more than just her cooking.

"It's not totally from scratch. I used a box cake mix, and added things like pudding, an extra egg, and olive oil."

He shook his head. "This is a box cake mix?"

"Yeah."

"I never would have thought about adding those to the mix. And the frosting?"

"I made it myself using heavy whipping cream, cocoa powder, powdered sugar, and other things."

"I saw the cake mix yesterday but never noticed the other items."

Her cheeks turned pink. "I ordered them on Monday. I wasn't sure how the week was going to go, so I planned different things to work with."

Blake polished off his dessert and set his plate aside, he took her empty plate and set it next to his.

"What would you like to do tonight?" He knew what he wanted to do. Kiss her, touch her, see how soft her skin was beneath her t-shirt.

She looked down at her hands, and Blake wondered at the shyness. When her head rose, he saw the need there. The want. He didn't say a word as he slid closer to her. His hand curved behind her neck and tugged her toward him. Her mouth turned up to his, and he captured her lips.

It wasn't enough. He wanted more, but he wouldn't go further without her agreement. Breaking the kiss, he ran his lips over her jaw and down her neck. "I want to touch you," he whispered.

"Yes, please." Her voice was soft and breathless.

Those words set his blood flowing. He pulled her t-shirt up until he found bare skin. She shivered when he touched her.

"Okay?"

"Oh yes."

He didn't hesitate. He pushed the fabric up until he could whip it over her head. He tossed the clothing aside, and looked down at Abby. Her skin was flushed, her breathing rapid, and her eyes wide.

The white lacy bra made his cock jump. Sexy but not overdone like other women he knew. Blake trailed his lips over the top of her breasts as his fingers found the front opening. The fabric loosened.

She started to raise her hands, but he glanced up at her, and she stopped. He nudged the fabric away. "So beautiful." Her breasts were full, her nipples taut and slightly darker. "Must taste."

His lips closed over her nipple. Abby moaned and arched into his embrace. Oh yes. He laved one nipple, then the other, enjoying her little moans of pleasure. His cock stiffened behind the fabric of his pants.

Yes, he wanted this woman, but he wouldn't rush her. Limited time with her or not. He wanted her ready. He leaned back as her hands found the bottom of his t-shirt, and she pulled it over his head.

Her nails lightly traced over his chest, sending a shaft of awareness through his body. "So hard," she whispered.

Pride welled in Blake. His workouts were so worth it for this moment with Abby. He captured her lips once again. This time, she kissed him back, their tongues dueling for power. Hands roaming over each other.

More, he wanted more. He slipped his hand over her belly to her pants. His fingers toyed with the waistband. Abby broke the kiss.

"Blake," she said her voice soft.

"Right here." He brushed his lips over her ear. Her skin was so soft against his. His finger dipped below her waist band.

A wail sounded through the apartment. In a flash, Abby was on her feet, grabbing her t-shirt and pulling it over her bare breasts. He was so deep in the lust zone it took a minute for Blake to realize Katie was screaming.

"Shh, what is it, sweetie?" He heard Abby's voice come through the baby monitor.

Blake stood and adjusted himself before walking into the bedroom. Abby had Katie on the bed, changing her diaper, but Katie wasn't happy.

"Is she okay?"

"A bad dream, maybe." She picked Katie up and began rocking her.

"Babies dream?"

"Some say yes, others say no." Abby rubbed Katie's back. "Let's see if she's hungry." He followed Abby into the kitchen where she warmed a bottle, and handed it to Katie. Who latched on like she'd never seen food before.

Blake just started at Katie. "She was hungry?"

"Looks like it." Abby smiled and sat down on the sofa to cradle Katie as she ate.

They were silent while Katie drank her bottle. When she was done. Abby burped her, but when she went to put her back to bed, Katie cried.

Blake started to pick her up, but Abby stopped him. "Let her be." She motioned him out of the room. He didn't like it, but he followed her lead. After several minutes,

Katie calmed down and became quiet.

"Is she asleep?" he asked.

"Maybe. Sometimes babies cry. Katie is a good baby, but tonight she's fussy. I'll stay out here for a while to make sure she gets to sleep before I go to bed."

"Or you could sleep with me." The words came out without him even thinking about them.

A startled blue gaze met his. "That's not a good idea."

"I think it's wonderful. We can take up where we left off." He took a step toward her.

"No, Blake." Abby held her hand up, and he stopped. "I shouldn't have let things get so out of control."

Color was high in her cheeks, and she crossed her arms over her chest, hiding her pert nipples from him. He wanted to reach for her, but she was practically folding inside herself.

"I'll respect your wishes." As much as his body craved hers, he wouldn't do anything about it tonight. Well, maybe a cold shower and taking himself in hand. Nothing with Abby. "Do you want some company?"

"I think it would be better if you go to bed."

He watched her pick up their plates and carry them

into the kitchen. He wanted to get her back out of her shell but wasn't sure how. Tomorrow was a brand new day, but time was running out. She was only here until Sunday. Blake picked up his shirt and her bra. He stood there for a moment, fingering the lace, wishing for something he wouldn't have tonight. For whatever reason, Abby wasn't ready. With a sigh, Blake laid her bra on the sofa before he went into his room. While there was so little time before Abby left, it didn't mean he couldn't see her afterward. That could be the key.

She'd said she was leery of being with him because she felt he was her employer. Once Katie was back with his sister, there would be no more employer/employee thinking. They could be just Blake and Abby. He shut his bedroom door and stripped as he walked to his bathroom, a wide smile on his face.

* * * *

Abby yawned. Even after Blake had gone to bed, she'd been awake for a long time. What had she been thinking last night, giving in to Blake? But it had been so good.

His hands on her skin. His touch, gentle yet firm, and

his kisses. She wanted more of them. *Stop it. You can't have him. He's a playboy.* Case in point: Right after breakfast this morning, he'd gotten a call from some woman. Abby could tell by the way his voice softened, and he disappeared into his bedroom, not his office, to take the call.

Abby shook her head. She didn't need the headache that would come from sleeping with Blake. Her body protested her thought. She ignored the longing in her gut. It was better this way. She'd only get her heart broken if she gave in to this overwhelming carnal lust.

Wanting to get some distance between her and Blake, she dressed Katie and left the apartment. When she was a block away and waiting for the light, she sent Blake a quick text to let him know she was taking Katie to the park.

It was warm today, and Abby was sweating a bit by the time they arrived. Katie had her usual time on the swing, and played in the woodchips. While Abby watched Katie, she heard the distant musical bells of what could only be an ice cream truck.

Sure enough, a moment later, the truck stopped on the street nearby. Abby scooped Katie up. Ice cream would be the perfect solution to help them cool off. With Katie in her stroller, she made her way to the truck, got a frozen yogurt, and found a spot under a tree for them.

After spreading out the blanket, she put Katie in the middle and sat down with the yogurt. Katie crawled into her lap and looked up expectedly.

"You're going to break someone's heart, Miss Katie." She scooped a little bit onto the spoon and into Katie's mouth.

Abby laughed at Katie's happy squeal. This was what made her job worth it. Seeing babies happy.

"I see you two are having fun."

Abby looked up to see Blake. Her mouth went dry. Not only was he wearing a t-shirt molded to his shoulders and chest, but a pair of running shorts, which showed off his long, lean legs.

"Hi, Blake."

"Hi. Ice cream, good idea. Be right back." Abby couldn't take her eyes away from him as he jogged to where the ice cream truck was parked. Her blood heated. Maybe sleeping with him wasn't such a bad idea.

She rolled her eyes. It was a bad idea, and one she

wouldn't entertain, but now she couldn't get the thought out of her head.

Blake returned with a popsicle and sat down beside her.

Katie started to reach for Blake, and he looked at Abby. "Can she have this?"

"It's better she doesn't. There's a lot of sugar in popsicles. Here, Katie." Abby scooped another spoonful of frozen yogurt into her mouth.

"And ice cream isn't." Blake gestured toward the bowl in Abby's hands.

"Frozen yogurt," she said with a grin. "Less sugar and good for her."

"Don't you eat things that are bad for you?"

"All the time. Look at dessert last night." Abby closed her eyes and silently swore. Why did she bring up last night?

Blake laughed. "True, but I like sweet things." He leaned over. "Your kisses are so sweet I want to try them again."

"Last night was a mistake." She gave Katie another bite.

"I don't think it was." He leaned closer to her.

"It's better we stay professional." Like she'd been acting professional? Well, most of the time she had.

Blake finished off his popsicle. He was turned toward her and propped himself up on his elbow. "I don't want to be professional with you." He ran his finger over her leg.

"That's all we can be." She had to resist him. No matter what her body wanted.

"Blake? Is that you?" A woman walked up to them. Abby noted her fashionable dress, and…high heels in a park. It was a miracle she hadn't broken an ankle.

"Hey, Lydia." Blake stood.

"What are you doing in the park?"

Lydia's eyes narrowed on Abby, and she smiled. Katie let out a squeal and crawled over to Blake, patting his leg with sticky hands.

"Yes, Miss Katie." He leaned down and picked Katie up before looking back at Lydia. "I'm enjoying a nice day with my niece."

"I didn't realize you had a niece." Lydia eyed Katie like the child was an anomaly.

"Yes. Where are my manners? Abby, this is Lydia;

Lydia, this is Abby."

"Hello." Abby kept a smile on her face.

Lydia looked down her nose at Abby, before she turned her gaze back to Blake. "I'm glad I ran into you. Dinner tonight?"

Abby sucked in a breath. While she shouldn't care if Blake went out with this woman, part of her did. She wanted him to say no. Begged him silently to turn the woman down. *He's a playboy. This is his type, not you.* The voice inside her was right. This was the type of woman Blake took out, the gossip columns proved that.

"Sorry, I'm taking care of Katie."

Abby barely prevented her mouth from dropping open.

"Isn't it her job?" Lydia pointed a finger at her.

Blake glanced over at Abby and grinned. "Yes, but I'm bonding with my niece, which means I need to spend time with her. Thank you for the offer, but not this week."

Abby noticed he left the invite open-ended. Smooth.

Lydia gave a huff. "Fine, maybe I'll call Scott to go out tonight."

"I'm sure he'll appreciate it." Blake kept his tone

light, but Abby heard the steel in it.

"Fine. Later." Lydia leaned forward to kiss Blake, and Katie squealed and hit Lydia in the cheek as she waved her arms. "Ouch. The child is a menace."

Abby put every ounce of her energy into suppressing the overwhelming urge to cheer Katie on. Barracudas like Lydia, now *those* were the real menaces.

Blake laughed, though Abby could tell it was a little forced.

"It was an accident." He took a step back as Katie waved her arms again.

"Sure." Lydia glared at Katie before she turned and walked away, her back straight and her head held high. She almost got away with her proud exit, except her heel sunk into the soft dirt, right up the arch, and she walked right out of it.

Glaring back at all of them now, Lydia wrenched her shoe from the grass and hobbled in one heel to the sidewalk. Once she got the other shoe on, she quickly disappeared around a corner.

Abby and Blake looked at each other, trying not to crack up, and lost the battle. Katie joined in and patted

Blake's cheek. "I'm not sure if I should thank you, sweetie, or wonder if you're protecting your uncle." He nuzzled Katie's neck.

"You're being good natured about this."

"She's a baby." He sat Katie on the blanket, and retook his seat, and pulled Katie into his lap. "Besides, she saved me."

"Saved you?" Abby's lips twitched.

"Yes. She's a barracuda, and I don't want to be bitten." His hazel eyes twinkled.

He'd used the same word she'd thought of to describe Lydia. Abby relaxed a bit.

"Unless it's you doing the biting."

Abby burst out laughing. "Sorry, I don't bite."

"Shame."

She could only shake her head at Blake. He broke down her defenses. In moments like this, when they were getting along and having fun, she could fall deeply for him. This man was dangerous. Very dangerous.

* * * *

Blake laid Katie in her bed. "Now, Miss Katie, I need you to sleep and let me have some quiet time with Abby tonight."

Katie laughed at him.

He leaned down and gave her a kiss before leaving the room. Abby was in the kitchen, and he wondered what she'd made for dessert. She'd surprised him tonight by making homemade pizza.

This woman really needed to be running her own restaurant. She'd make a fortune. Everything she cooked was delicious. It wasn't he was a picky eater, but he knew what he liked. And he'd enjoyed all of the meals so far and would again if he could.

When they arrived home from the park, she'd put Katie down for a nap, and disappeared into the kitchen. Later, she played with Katie, and he watched. She was so good with his niece. Heck, she was probably good with all kids.

"Want to watch a movie?" he asked when she came out of the kitchen with bowls in her hands.

"Sure. Which one are you thinking of?"

He had multiple streaming services he'd told her she could use at any time. So far, he'd only seen her use one to show Katie an animated series. His go-to shows were disaster movies, his second was action/adventure. He pulled up one of his favorite action/adventure movies.

"Okay?"

"Yes. I love this movie." She handed him a bowl. He looked at the contents. "Brownie, covered with caramel sauce and dulce de leche ice cream."

"If you tell me you made the ice cream, I'm going to go crazy."

She laughed. "Ice cream, no. The brownie, yes."

Blake dipped his spoon in and took a bite. The ice cream was creamy. The brownie, though. Wow. It melted on his tongue in chocolate and caramel bliss.

Abby took a bite of hers as the movie started. They ate in silence. When Abby finished, he took her bowl and carried both into the kitchen. When he returned, he turned the lights down and sat so his thigh touched hers. Even minimal touch set him on fire. He wanted this woman like he'd never wanted anyone before.

Abby shifted but didn't get up and move away. He took it as a good sign. He tried to watch the movie, but her heat called to him. He stretched his arm out and over her shoulder.

"Maybe I should go to bed," she said.

"I didn't mean to make you uncomfortable." He removed his arm. The last thing he wanted to do was make her uneasy.

"You didn't." She turned and faced him. "Us being together isn't a good idea."

"Why not?" He really wanted to know what she was thinking.

"Because I'm the nanny."

"So?"

She shook her head. "I don't know how to explain it any better than I have before."

"Try." He waited, but she stayed silent. "I'm attracted to you, Abby. I want to see where this attraction leads. I don't care if you're the nanny, work in a grocery store, or anything else. I've seen a woman who cares about children, who believes in her job, and is a damn fantastic cook. I like talking to you too. You have good insights. I want to get to know you better. Much better."

"I…" Her eyes widened, and there was panic in them. "I'm sorry." She jumped up and ran for her bedroom.

Blake thought about following her but decided not to.

He had Saturday and Sunday to convince her they could be together.

"Oh Abby, what are you thinking?"

Blake turned around, but he didn't see Abby. He realized her voice was coming from the baby monitor.

"He's not the man for you." Her voice was soft, but he heard it loud and clear.

He should walk away, or at least let her know, but he didn't. She was fighting against them being together and maybe this would give him some insight why.

"I don't know, Katie. Your uncle is a sexy man, and any woman would be happy to jump in bed with him. I just can't."

Interesting. She said *can't*, not *won't*. It also made him happy she thought him sexy.

"I don't know. Maybe I should throw caution to the wind, but could I live with myself? My life is finally at the point where I can realize my dream. I don't want anything to mess it up."

A ring tone sounded. It wasn't his phone, it was Abby's. "Hey, Sis, what's up?"

Blake walked into his bedroom. He wouldn't

eavesdrop on her private conversation with her sister. As he laid in bed, he thought about what Abby had said. They only had one more full night together. She was attracted to him; that was a plus.

He stared at the ceiling. Why was it so important to him to get her into bed? Maybe because he wanted to show her there was more to him than what she was seeing. He wanted to show her the loving man he was at his core, the man he never showed to anyone.

Now to figure out how to do that.

* * * *

Abby groaned as Katie giggled in her bed. Time to get up. She didn't want to. Sleep had been elusive last night, and she was still tired. "Be right there, Miss Katie."

Rolling out of bed and to her feet, Abby went into the bathroom, splashed water on her face, brushed her teeth and dressed. There were faint circles under her eyes. She shrugged. Not much she could do about them. When she went back in the room, Blake was there.

Her heart pounded. He looked well rested, the rat.

"I heard Katie and saw the bathroom door was closed," he said, laying Katie on the bed and beginning to undress her.

"I can take care of her." Her words were defensive, and she wanted to apologize.

Blake turned his head and grinned. "It's fine." Abby watched as he expertly changed Katie's diaper and redressed her. "All done." He lifted Katie into his arm. "I've made coffee. I wasn't sure what you have planned for breakfast, but we could go out and give you a break."

Abby blinked. Who was this man? "I made a cinnamon coffee cake for this morning; it just needs to bake."

"Can it wait until tomorrow?" His tone was eager.

"I guess."

"Good." He bounced Katie in his arms, and she giggled. "Why don't you pack up Katie's diaper bag, and I'll get her dressed. There's a great little café down the street."

"But…" she started.

"No buts. You deserve at least one meal off, now scoot." He motioned with his free hand, and somehow Abby found herself obeying him. Maybe it was a good idea to get out of the apartment where it was just the three of them.

At least in public she wouldn't want to throw herself at him. Or that's what she told herself.

* * * *

The café was a trendy place. Lots of people, but they didn't have to wait for a table. The waitress fussed over Katie when they sat down. Coffee, water, and juice were brought while Abby looked over the menu.

She didn't eat out much, but when she did, she studied the menu for ideas and to see what other places had to offer. Although Scrumptious Addictions wasn't a mom and pop type of place, it wasn't upscale either.

Katie pounded on the high chair tray. "Goodness." Abby pulled out Katie's sippy cup and a handful of dry cereal for her.

"How do you always know what she wants?" Blake asked.

"I don't. But since she hasn't had breakfast, I figured she's hungry and probably a little thirsty." Abby shut her menu.

"Are you ready to order?" the bubbly blonde waitress asked.

"What do you recommend?" Abby asked.

The waitress' eyes widened. Maybe it wasn't a question she got often. "Depends on what you want. The waffles are great. If you're looking for more protein, eggs with bacon or sausage. The breakfast sandwiches are a quick meal."

Abby considered the waitress' suggestions. "I'd like scrambled eggs, with bacon and hash browns well done. Whole wheat toast, and one waffle with an extra bowl for the baby."

"You got it. Sir?"

Blake blinked. "I'll have the pancake special with sausage."

"Coming right up." The waitress left.

"That's a lot of food," he said.

"I'll be sharing with Miss Katie here." Abby grabbed the sippy cup before it fell off the tray and put it on the table.

"What will you do once this job is done?" Blake asked.

Abby considered her answer. "Well, since I was supposed to be on vacation this week, I'll take my vacation and go from there." Not really a lie, she would be on vacation from the agency but working at the restaurant.

Blake's eyes widened. "They called you in from your vacation? I'm so sorry; you should have told me."

"Why?" Abby shrugged. "You needed a nanny, and I was the only one available."

"But you were on vacation. I can't believe there wasn't anyone else."

She laughed. "Blake, nannies are not a dime a dozen. It takes training, and most of us have specific hours we work. There are only a few who take on 24/7 jobs. I usually don't anymore."

"I'm honored you did for me."

"I was doing my boss a favor." At least, that's what she told herself. She didn't mention Blake paying four times the normal amount was a consideration. He had to know it was part of the decision.

"I'm glad you took the job." He reached across the table and ran his fingers over the back of her hand. "You're so good with Katie. We're both going to miss you."

Abby's skin tingled where Blake touched her. She gently withdrew her hand from his touch. "I doubt that."

"I'm going to miss this little of bundle of energy too." He tickled Katie's cheek, and she laughed. "Why?"

"Why what?"

"Why don't you think I'll miss you?"

"I'm just the hired help. Just wait until Katie starts to walk." She deflected the conversation away from her.

"God help me."

He took the bait, and Abby couldn't help herself. A belly laugh erupted, and Blake joined her.

"You can't blame me. I can barely handle her crawling."

The waitress walked up with their food and set it on the table, made sure they didn't need anything else, and walked away.

Abby put some of her eggs in the bowl for Katie, along with some waffle. Katie dug in. They ate in silence. Abby realized how comfortable she was with Blake. Yes, he had money, but he didn't flaunt it. Well, except for the "buy anything you need for the baby" thing, and she couldn't fault him for wanting to take care of his niece.

The restaurant, for example, wasn't some upscale place, but a local small business and, thankfully, not a chain. That's why she wanted to work at Scrumptious Addictions. It was local and not a chain.

Abby was cleaning up Katie when an older woman came up to the table. "I'm sorry to disturb you, but I wanted to say how nice it is to see a couple out together with their child. And such a well-behaved baby."

Abby opened her mouth to correct the woman's assumption, but Blake jumped in.

"Thank you. That's very kind of you."

The woman smiled and walked away.

"Why didn't you correct her?" Abby asked. While she hadn't corrected others who thought she was Katie's mom and Blake her husband, when she'd been mistaken for the mother of a child in her care on other jobs, she'd gently corrected the person. What made Blake and Katie so different?

"Because she was being nice, and I didn't feel the need. Besides…" A flash went off by their table, temporarily blinding Abby, and Katie wailed as a young man raced from the restaurant. Blake leaped up, but it was too late. The man was gone.

"Easy, sweetheart." Abby stood up and pulled Katie

from the high chair, her own legs wobbling. Blake steadied her with a hand around her waist, and the comfort she drew from his touch warmed her. "Who was he, Blake?"

"Not here. I have an idea, but let's talk at home."

The waitress rushed over. "I'm so sorry. We didn't realize what he was up to."

Blake waved his hand. "Not your problem." He pulled out his wallet and handed her some money. "Keep the change." He turned to Abby. "Are you okay to walk?"

"Y-yes."

"Let's go. I'll get the diaper bag and stroller; you handle Katie."

Abby nodded, talking softly to Katie as she walked out of the restaurant. Katie hiccupped as Abby cleared the door. "Did the man scare you?" She was still trying to make sense of what happened.

The absolute fury crossed Blake's face shocked her. He wiped it away quickly, but she'd seen it.

He came out and unfolded the stroller. Abby settled Katie into the stroller and strapped her in. Thankfully, Katie was over her scare and settled right into the seat. "Let's go." Blake started walking at a fast clip.

Oh yes, he was still angry. While he wasn't showing it on his face, it was obvious in the way he walked, fast and with purpose, and his knuckles were white where he gripped the stroller. When they arrived at the apartment, he put the diaper bag on the counter and took Katie out of the stroller and placed her on the floor.

"I need to go into my office for a bit." He left before Abby could ask a single question.

"I think someone is beyond angry," she said to Katie.

* * * *

"I don't fucking care it's Saturday. Get him on the phone now!" Blake paced around his office while he waited for his CFO to get the owner of the gossip rag on the phone. He'd recognized the photographer and was pissed the man managed to get a picture of Abby and Katie.

Five minutes later, his CFO came back on the line. "Daryl is on the line."

"Daryl, I want any photos your photographer took in the next hour, or I'll sue you for everything you have."

"Come on, Blake. It's Saturday."

"I don't give a damn. He invaded not only my privacy

but others at the restaurant who did not consent to his intrusion. I've told you before: At events, I'm fair game, but not in private. And if this is what you are stooping to now, you haven't learned how nasty I can fight."

"You can't blame us for trying."

Heat invaded Blake from his toes to the roots of his hair. "Jeff, get our lawyers on the phone so we can get an injunction now."

"There's no need for lawyers," Daryl sputtered.

"Jordan Frost here."

"Jordan, Blake. I'm having an issue. Daryl from the *Seattle Tattle* is here, along with Jeff."

"What happened?"

Blake outlined quickly what happened. He knew Jordan from some charity events he and his fiancée, Crystal, had attended. They went back years to when Jordan was just starting out. Blake had quickly put him on retainer. The man was brilliant.

"I see. Daryl, we've sent you cease and desist letters, which you have obviously ignored, and we have active restraining orders against at least two photographers who regularly sell images to you. Blake, Jeff, give me an hour, and I'll have your injunction."

"That isn't necessary," Daryl sputtered.

"Actually, it is," Jordan said. "Blake, I'll call you when I have it."

Blake blew out a breath. "Jeff?"

"Still here."

"I am too," Daryl said. "Give me fifteen minutes to talk with the photographer." There was silence.

"You still here, Jeff?"

"Yep. I'll work with Jordan if he needs me. We'll get this taken care of."

"Thanks." Blake ran his hand through his hair. He needed to talk Abby just in case things didn't go his way, but he wouldn't do it until he knew if the photo would show up or not. It was going to be a long hour.

Chapter 7

Blake walked out of his office an hour and a half later. Abby had put Katie down for a nap, and he found her sitting on the sofa, scrolling through recipes on her tablet.

"All done?" She closed her tablet and set it on the coffee table.

"Yes." He sat down beside her. "I'm sorry about disappearing. I needed to take care of that photographer."

Abby's eyes widened. "All of this is about a picture?"

"Yes." He sighed. "The photographer was from the *Seattle Tattle*. I have an agreement with them, at events or parties, I don't care if they take pictures of me, but in private, that's not allowed."

"So what he did today violated the agreement."

He nodded. "I needed to nip it in the bud. Which is why I disappeared."

"And you got it settled?"

"I did. It took the threat of an emergency injunction from a judge."

"I didn't think you could do that."

"When you have a good lawyer you can." Blake took Abby's hand. "It shouldn't have happened. You have a right to privacy and shouldn't be dragged into it and neither should Katie."

"Explain to me why this was so bad?"

Blake blinked. "It was an invasion of privacy."

"I get it. I don't get why you were so upset over it."

Did she not understand? Abby wasn't naïve. She had to understand what it meant. No, there was something else at play here, but what?

"You weren't upset your picture was taken?"

"Not in the moment, but your reaction was instantaneous. I'm curious why."

"Because this could have caused you problems."

Abby tilted her head and stared at him. "I don't see how."

"Abby, you know who I am, right?" Had he met a woman who had no clue who he was?

"I read a couple of articles about you and your company after I got here. I know you're a rich playboy."

"I hate being called a playboy."

"Sorry." She looked contrite. "Was being photographed with the nanny an issue?"

"Hell no." She didn't get it. "Abby, the press could make your life hell. They would follow you everywhere all because of one photo."

"If they saw us at breakfast, without the photo, couldn't they do it anyway?"

"I guess they could." He'd never thought of it like that.

"It's not that I don't appreciate you trying to protect me, but Katie is more important. Besides, I lead a very boring life; anyone following me would get bored in less than a day."

"You've encountered this before, haven't you?" Why hadn't he thought of it? Abby had seemed calm, a little unsteady, but calm, her first instinct had been Katie, not the photographer or what he had done.

"Yes." She squeezed his fingers before moving her hand away. "I work for people from all walks of life and have been photographed before. I'm not happy the photo was taken, but Katie's upset was the most important thing right now."

"What have you done when this has happened before?"

"I do my best to shelter my charges. Parents don't always warn me, but I do keep an eye out. My attention wasn't where it needed to be this morning, and I feel guilty."

Blake was floored. She felt guilty? "You have nothing to feel guilty about."

"We were out together with Katie. I'm usually more on guard, but I let it slip today, and this happened."

"I did too." When he thought back to the last few days, he'd let his guard slip with Abby several times, allowing her to see him, not the man he projected to the world. And it didn't bother him at all. Interesting. An ache began low in the gut. He pushed away the pain. Abby wouldn't hurt him. She was too kind-hearted.

"We both learned from this morning. What is going to happen now?"

"Not only do I have assurances the photo will not be published, my lawyer was able to get an emergency injunction until we go to court next week."

"What happens?"

"They can't publish before the hearing, and if the judge agrees, they have to turn all the photos, negatives, and/or digital media to me so I can destroy it."

"And if he doesn't?"

"Then they can publish it." He sucked in a breath. "But if they do publish, they know I'll come after them with everything I have."

"Don't."

"Excuse me."

"Blake, it isn't worth the hassle, unless they got a picture of Katie. One picture of me isn't going to hurt. Unless you don't want a picture of you and me together, however innocent. I just feel it isn't worth the battle."

"You view things so differently."

She shook her head. "I grew up with a mother who checked out when it came to her children. You wonder why I became a nanny. The reason is money. I have a younger brother and sister, and I raised them because my mother couldn't be bothered."

Blake froze. His mother hadn't checked out; she had kept them fed, clothed, and a roof over their heads, and she'd worked very hard to keep her kids safe. Abby's life was different. "My mom worked two jobs but never neglected us kids."

"All my mom could see was the next sugar daddy who'd take care of her." She shook her head. "It doesn't matter anymore. The thing is, if I let one photo bother me, I'd never have made it through life."

"What do your brother and sister do?" He wanted to know more about her family, and since she was talking, he wanted to encourage her.

"My brother is in the military. He loves it. My sister is graduating from college in a few months with a degree in finance."

"You've worked as a nanny to put her through school."

"Yes, and to put myself through school too."

"There's a nanny school?"

Abby laughed, and his mood lightened. "I took community college courses and became a nanny through them. But my passion is cooking, as if you hadn't noticed. I put myself through culinary school."

His jaw dropped open. He shouldn't be surprised, but he was. "I kept thinking you should open your own restaurant.”

“No, I don't want the hassle.”

“Why haven't you gone to work for someone?”

“I won't sugar coat it. Money. Starting out, the salary is pretty low, and there was no way I could pay for my sister's college, let alone my own degree. I didn't want to have massive debt, so the nanny job.”

“Couldn't you get scholarships?” He made a mental note to check in with Jeff. While he made sure he gave back to community, he was starting to see a gap.

“It was difficult for me. My sister got several, which helped us both. I didn't mind. I've had my goal in mind for years.”

“How close are you?”

“Very.”

He opened his mouth, but she held her hand up.

“Don't offer help. It's kind of you, but no. I've been determined since I was fourteen to make my own way in the world, and I will do it.”

“You will.” He understood the drive and her need to do it herself. Hadn't he been that way? Hell, he still was.

“So now you know, let's put what happened this

morning out of our minds."

"How long will Katie be asleep?" Before she could answer, his cell rang. He glanced at the display. His mother. "Excuse me, I have to take this." Abby nodded and strode across the room. "What's up, Mom?"

"Hi, sweetheart. I was wondering if you would bring Katie by for a visit. I'd really like to see her and meet this nanny." He glanced at Abby. "Let me check." He placed the phone against his chest. "My mother would like Katie to visit."

Abby glanced at her phone. "She'll be asleep another twenty minutes, and she'll need to eat a bit before you can take her."

"That will work." He put the phone back up to his ear. "How about we arrive around two, an hour and a half from now."

"Great, darling. It's before my therapy appointment. See you in a bit."

Blake put his phone back in his pocket. "Okay, we have someplace to be in a bit."

"You mean you and Katie do."

He shook his head. "You too. My mom wants to meet

you."

"Me?" Her voice squeaked. "Why me?"

"She only said she wanted to meet the nanny taking care of her granddaughter. But it still gives me time." He walked to the front door.

"For what?"

He grinned. "My secret. But keep your evening free." He stood. "I'm going to run out for a bit, but I'll be back by one-thirty to pick you and Katie up."

"Okay."

Blake grinned as he left the apartment. His mother's request gave him the time he needed. Tonight, he was going to go all out and seduce Abby. At least he hoped he could. Because he wanted to show her in more than one way he cared.

* * * *

Abby took a deep breath as they walked into the rehab unit. Blake explained his mom was here until next week, after which, he'd hired a home health nurse to care for her until her foot was completely healed.

If she didn't know already what a good family guy Blake was, this showed her. First, he took his niece because his mother was injured, and he paid for her to have a home health nurse. Abby also suspected his mother was receiving the best care money could buy.

Katie was babbling away as they stopped by the nurses' station.

"Mr. Ellington, good to see you again."

"Thank you. We're going to visit my mother. Is there any issue with a ten-month-old baby?"

"All we ask is you don't let her run up and down the hallways."

"Not a problem." Blake looked at Abby and grinned before taking her arm and guiding her down the hall.

"Hey, Mom," Blake said as he walked into the room.

Abby smiled at the gray haired woman sitting in the chair next to the bed. "Mrs. Ellington," she said.

"Gma, Gma," Katie called out and began struggling in the stroller.

"Easy." Abby knelt down, unfastened Katie, pulled her into her arms and carried over to Blake's mother. "Gentle, Katie." Abby set Katie into Mrs. Ellington's lap.

"Oh my! I swear she's grown."

"She probably has," Blake commented. "Abby is a

miracle worker."

Abby lowered her eyes as her face heated.

"I forgot to introduce you two. Mom, as you probably know by now, this is Abby from Practically Perfect Nannies. Abby, my mom, Maggie Ellington."

"It's a pleasure to meet you," Abby said. Outside of her foot in a boot, Maggie Ellington looked strong and healthy.

"I can't thank you enough for helping out Blake. He had no clue what he was getting into when I asked him to babysit." Maggie cuddled Katie, who cooed while resting her head against Maggie's shoulder.

"It's no problem."

"Blake, why don't you go find a chair so you can sit down." She gestured to the lone empty chair in the room.

Blake hesitated, then shrugged. "Be right back."

"Please, sit down," Ms. Ellington said as he left the room.

Abby sat down but kept her gaze on Katie. The baby seemed perfectly happy to lay against her grandmother's shoulder.

"I meant what I said, Abby. May I call you Abby?"

"Of course."

"I'm Maggie. Blake had no clue. It was a good thing I'd slipped the nanny agency card in the diaper bag."

"It was a little touch and go when I arrived." Her lips tilted up.

"Oh? Tell me."

"Well, poor Katie had diarrhea."

"How did Blake handle the little pooper?"

"Not well." Abby went on to explain what she experienced when she arrived.

Maggie started giggling, which caused Katie to laugh, and Abby joined in. Blake strode back into the room with a chair and a concerned look. "Having fun?"

Maggie waved her hand for him to sit down. "Abby was telling me about what happened when she arrived."

Blake glared at her, and Abby smiled back. "It was pretty funny."

"Now maybe, but not at the time." He crossed his arms over his chest.

"Poor Blake. I'm just grateful it was you, Abby, and not that horrid woman he's been dating. Vanessa something the other."

"Mom," Blake started.

"Don't 'mom' me, young man."

Abby glanced at Blake. His face had turned a light red, and he nodded to his mother. "Yes, ma'am," he said.

Respect for Blake went up several notches. A man who didn't argue with his mother.

"The one time you brought her over to the house, all she could see were dollar signs. I heard her complain I wasn't living in the right neighborhood."

Was Vanessa one of the women who'd called Blake? She wasn't the woman at the park. Just how many women was he dating? Not it was any of her business. She was Katie's nanny, and she'd best remember that.

Just before three, Katie began to get fussy. Abby took her from Maggie. "I think someone is getting too fussy for an extended visit."

"It's okay," Maggie said. "My physical therapist will be here shortly for more torture."

"Mom, if they're not treating you right..." Blake stood.

His mother waved her hands. "They're treating me just fine. You don't need to be so protective of me, honey."

"I can't help it."

His tone was soft, and Abby found herself softening toward Blake. He truly cared about his mother and how she was being treated. Why did it surprised her, she didn't know. Maybe because her own mother had abandoned her and her siblings.

"It was great meeting you, Maggie," she said after she got Katie settled back into the stroller.

"You, too, my dear."

"I'll wait by the elevator while you say good-bye." Abby pushed Katie out of the room. It was going to take some time to process what she'd witnessed between Blake and his mother. Abby had never been around a mothering influence such as Maggie. It was also obvious Blake loved his mother and would do anything for her. Abby's thoughts chased each other around in her brain.

The drive home was uneventful. Katie fell asleep as soon as Blake started driving. He insisted on carrying Katie up to the apartment and putting her in her crib. He told her he had an errand to run. But he wanted her to rest and not to worry about dinner; he had it covered.

* * * *

Abby read the text on her phone yet again.

Remember, no cooking. I have a surprise for you.

Blake had sent the text an hour after he left the apartment. Abby couldn't help wondering what he was up to. She'd already taken care of all the laundry and tidied up around the apartment. Sadness enveloped her when she thought of moving on tomorrow. It wasn't unusual for her to be sad when leaving a charge, but she'd push through it.

She'd learned early on she couldn't stay with every client, and it actually was better to move around, but Katie had wormed her way into her heart, and if Abby was honest with herself, so had Blake.

Maybe it was a good thing tomorrow was her last day. If she stayed much longer, she was worried her willpower to resist Blake would disappear. She'd just finished feeding Katie her dinner when the apartment door opened.

"Miss Abby," Walter, the concierge, called out.

"Come on in." Abby handed Katie her sippy cup and stood to see Walter directing people into the kitchen area. "What's all this?"

"Mr. Ellington asked me to let them in and to tell you you're not to touch anything."

Abby shook her head. "Crazy man," she whispered.

Trays lined the counter, and with a wave, Walter followed them out of the apartment. "Well, Katie, your uncle has something up his sleeve."

Abby took care of Katie's dishes, bathed the baby and put her into her playpen for a bit. Tempted to check out what was on the counter, she took a step toward the kitchen and stopped when the front door opened.

Blake walked in with a bouquet of flowers in a very decorative vase. "Aha! You were going to peak?"

Heat crept over her neck and face, and Blake laughed.

"I'm glad you didn't." He walked over and set the flowers on the counter. "These are for you."

"You brought me flowers?" Her heart pounded as she looked at the beautiful arrangement. White carnations, yellow and pink tulips, dark pink peonies, white dogwood, and magnolia. "You didn't have to."

"I wanted to. Beautiful flowers for a beautiful woman."

Her face grew even warmer. Katie giggled and held her arms up when Blake approached the playpen. "How is my Katie?" He picked her up and nuzzled her neck. Katie cooed and yawned. "Bedtime."

"I'll take her." Abby tried to gather her scattered thoughts.

"I'll put her down. Katie and I are going to have a little talk." He picked up the baby monitor and walked into the bedroom.

Abby wondered what he was going to talk to Katie about, it wasn't like Katie had an extensive vocabulary. She turned back to the flowers and ran her finger over the soft petals of the carnations. When was the last time a man brought her flowers? Her family didn't count. Her brother always sent her flowers on her birthday. This was different.

Blake came out of the bedroom with the baby monitor, walked into his bedroom, came back out a minute later in bare feet. He set the monitor on the coffee table. "Katie is down for the night. It's our time."

She swallowed. "Our time?"

"Yes." He guided her to the dining room table and held a chair out for her. Abby sat down, perplexed at what Blake was doing. "I'll be right back."

She kept her gaze on him as he went into the kitchen.

His back was to her as he opened the containers which had arrived earlier. What had he done?

"Close your eyes," he said.

"I'm not sure this is a good idea."

"Please, Abby. I want to surprise you."

The plea tugged at her heart. She closed her eyes and concentrated on hearing him. Soft footfalls from the kitchen to the table and the clink of glasses and utensils being set on the table alerted her to where he was.

Blake retreated and returned. The smell of perfectly seared beef reached her nose. Her stomach growled. "Someone is hungry. Open your eyes."

Abby's gaze took in the plate sitting in front of her. Prime rib, a baked potato, and zucchini. A breadbasket sat on the table, along with wine glasses and a bottle of Bordeaux. "This looks so good."

"I took a guess on how done you liked your meat based on how you cooked this week."

"I'm sure it's fine."

Blake picked up the wine bottle and poured into the wine glasses, and held his up. "To Abby, the nanny I didn't know I needed."

She giggled as they clinked glasses, and she took a sip of the full-bodied wine. After setting her wine glass down, she sliced into the meat. "Why the special meal?" she asked before she slid the fork into her mouth. Abby was unable to stop the moan of pleasure at the perfectly cooked prime rib.

"It's your last night with me."

His words sent a zing of anticipation through her. "And Katie." She had no idea why she felt the need to remind him.

"Of course. Eat."

They ate in companionable silence. Abby thoroughly enjoyed the food. "Where did you get this?"

"I'm hurt you didn't think I cooked it."

Her laughter filled the room. "I was here when it was delivered, and you were the one who said you never cooked."

"You got me. I went to the Prime Rib House."

"They're the best ones in the northwest." She remembered the time she worked there as a fill-in cook. It got boring fast, but others loved it.

When Blake went to refill her wine glass, she shook

her head. "One is enough." She usually didn't drink on the job, but she hadn't been able to refuse.

"I noticed you only drink water or juice." He put the wine bottle down.

"A glass of wine now and again is fine. Having a child to take care of, it's good not to get in the habit."

"I can understand that." He stood and began to clear the dishes. Abby pushed her chair out to stand. "Sit. I'll take care of this."

He was being very considerate, she thought. But there was more to it. There was a sparkle in his eyes she'd not seen before. "Why don't we adjourn to the sofa," he said, walking over to her and holding out his hand.

She allowed herself to indulge him. Before she sat down, she kicked off her shoes. Once on the sofa, she glanced over at him, and he was looking at her. "Now what?"

"That's up to you." He turned to her. "I want to kiss you, Abby. Actually, I want more than to kiss you."

She swallowed. Katie was asleep, and Abby was tired of fighting herself. It was their last night together, and it wasn't like they'd see each other again. Tomorrow, they'd part ways, so why not indulge herself?

"I'd like it too."

"Are you sure?"

"I am."

"I'll stop if you ask me, but I need to know now—is this what you want?"

"Oh, Blake." Her heart melted. He was trying to protect her. "I want to be with you."

Desire flared in his eyes before he cupped the back of her neck and drew her to him.

Their lips met in a soft kiss, he drew her closer, and her lips parted to his. She could faintly taste the butter from dinner.

The need welled in her, faster than she'd ever known before. All thought about him being a playboy and his money fled her mind, and she concentrated on this moment. Being in his arms and with him.

One night wouldn't hurt, would it?

* * * *

Blake held Abby lightly in his arms. She wasn't pulling away. She was kissing him back, and her arms held him tight. Hunger flared in his belly. Hunger for Abby. She had no idea how sexy she looked in her standard jeans and Practically Perfect Nannies t-shirt.

He wasn't sure she was even aware of the little moans she made when she ate, especially tonight. Stopping at the Prime Rib House had been his best idea. He'd thought about stopping and getting dessert but decided he wanted her for dessert.

She'd finally opened up to him after breakfast, telling him more about herself. Abby shifted, and Blake brought his thoughts back to the moment. She fit perfectly in his arms. He wanted her in is bed.

Breaking the kiss, he gazed down at her dreamy eyes. "Shall we take this into my bedroom?"

At her nod, he stood and pulled her to her feet. He grabbed the baby monitor and led her into his bedroom. Blake kept his gaze on Abby. He wanted to see his private domain through her eyes. He wasn't the person the gossip rags dragged through the mud on a regular basis. He wanted more than anything for her to understand he was so much more.

"Very nice," she murmured.

"What were you expecting?" He put the baby monitor

on the nightstand and turned to her.

"More glitzy, maybe. But I like the soft browns and beiges."

He nodded. He'd done the bedroom himself. "Would you believe me if I said you're the first woman I've had in my bedroom outside of family."

Her eyes widened.

"It's true." He leaned down and kissed her cheek. "Regardless of what the gossip pages say, I'm not the playboy they make me out to be." His fingers worked at the t-shirt fabric and pulled it from the waistband of her jeans.

Her cheeks were pink, and he wasn't sure if it was from his touch or what he'd just told her. At the moment, he didn't care. He wanted her in his bed, underneath him. He whipped the t-shirt over her head.

White lace cupped her breasts. He kissed the tops of her breasts and heard her sigh. Blake glanced up.

"I want to undress you," she whispered.

Straightening, he dropped his hands to his sides. "Be my guest." Her fingers brushed his chest, and his cock jumped. Maybe this wasn't such a good idea if a little touch sent a shaft of pleasure through his body.

But he forced himself to stand still as she drew his polo shirt over his head and ran her fingers over his chest.

"So hard. You work out every day, don't you?"

"I do." Because his job required him to be either behind his computer or in meetings, he made sure he exercised. "You rarely sit still."

She tilted her head up and grinned. "When you take care of kids, the only down time one gets is when they're sleeping."

"That explains why my sister always looks tired." He had a new appreciation for his sister and his mother. "My turn."

His fingers found the button and zipper on her jeans and undid them. Gooseflesh popped out as he lowered the zipper and pushed her jeans down. The woman had long, toned legs. "Do you work out?"

She giggled. "Only if you consider running after kids working out."

"It could be." He remembered playing with Katie and how she never seemed to run out of energy. Abby stepped out of her pants as he straightened. Her fingers were at his jeans.

Her touch was less firm than his. Her fingers trembled, and he started to worry. When she fumbled with the zipper, his fingers closed over hers. Abby glanced up at him.

"If you don't want to do this, tell me."

"Oh no. I want this. I'm just a little nervous."

"Why?" Her words made him curious.

Her cheeks turned a dark red. "It's been a while for me."

Her declaration surprised him. She was a beautiful, sexy woman. "If I move too fast, tell me. I don't want you to be uncomfortable." He gritted his teeth and mentally recited football stats to keep himself from rushing her.

"Thank you." The zipper on his jeans lowered, and she peeled the fabric down. Her fingers lightly grazed his erection. While she was bent over, she slid her socks off then straightened.

Blake stared at her. While her face was pink, she licked her lips, and her eyes gleamed with need. He brushed a kiss against her lips as his hands reached for the ever-present ponytail she kept her hair in.

He worked the band off and her blonde hair—soft and

faintly smelling of strawberries—cascaded over his fingers. Blake tossed the band toward the baby monitor, not caring where it landed.

"Absolutely beautiful," he whispered as he ran his fingers through her hair. "Why do you keep it up?"

"It's easy, and this way, babies like Katie don't pull it."

He winced, remembering the first time Katie grabbed a handful of his hair. "Not a bad idea." He pressed a kiss against her temple as he unfastened her lace bra and tossed it aside. A shiver went through her body as he ushered her to his bed.

"I want to worship you," he murmured against her skin as he guided her onto his bed and joined her. Damn, she looked good in his bed with her hair spread on his pillow, fanning out over the soft fabric.

He kissed his way from her cheeks to her breasts. Her nipples were delightfully erect and pink, as if begging for his attention. He placed a soft kiss on one then the other, before covering one with his hand and the other with his lips.

Abby groaned and arched, pushing herself into his

mouth and hand. Blake switched breasts, and Abby slid her hands over his back, her nails lightly tracing his spine. After giving attention to her breasts, he slid south and hooked his finger into her underwear.

She lifted her butt off the bed as he slid her panties down, his lips caressing her skin as he flung the fabric away once it was free of her feet.

The sweet smell of arousal hit him. He wanted to give her everything he had, but his cock was pulsing with need, and he didn't know how long he was going to last.

"Someone is overdressed." Her fingers caressed his erection through the fabric of his briefs.

"I can fix that." He swept his own underwear off.

"Oh my," she said, her eyes going to his dick before her fingers closed over it. "Hard and ready."

"I have been for a while."

A shy smile formed on her lips. "Come to me, lover."

"With pleasure." Blake reached over to the nightstand and grabbed a condom. He sheathed himself and covered her body with his before taking her mouth in a hard kiss.

* * * *

Abby didn't know where those sexy words came

from. All she knew was she wanted Blake. He was so considerate of her, putting a condom on without her having to ask, and turned her on even more. She was on birth control, but he didn't know about it, so she appreciated him taking the lead. Yet another side to this complicated man.

His kiss threw all thoughts out of her mind, leaving only the feeling of his skin against hers. She wanted him so much. She didn't want to wait.

"Please," she said against his lips as she squirmed and opened her legs.

"As you wish." He shifted and his cock was at her entrance. "So ready for me." He moved his hips.

Her lashes fluttered shut as he penetrated her. Slowly. Inch by inch, her body accepted him until he was seated fully in her pussy.

She opened her mouth and let out a big breath.

"Are you okay?" he asked.

"Fine. But you need to move."

He laughed and pulled back to thrust back home a second later.

"Yes." Her nails dug into his lower back as he began to move within her. It might have been a while, but her body knew the right dance. Nerve endings came alive and pulsed within her. It didn't take long until she went over the top and climaxed. Small shudders were still going through her body when his lips captured hers. Blake took away what little breath she had left.

Tonight was for them. Tomorrow, they'd part ways, and Abby would always remember the feel of him within her.

Chapter 8

Abby's eyes fluttered open, and she gasped. She was back in her bedroom. How did that happen? The last thing she remembered was Blake waking her early this morning and making love to her once again.

A giggle made her glance toward the crib. Katie was awake. Abby got out of bed and groaned. Muscles hurt in places she'd forgotten about. She took a very quick shower and got dressed, now she could attended to Katie.

When she opened the bedroom door, she heard voices. Low, but there. Taking a deep breath, Abby walked out with Katie on her hip. Blake, two women, and another man sat at the dining table.

"Ma, ma, ma," Katie babbled, wiggling in Abby's hold.

"Katie!" The brown haired woman jumped up and ran over to where Abby stood with Katie.

Katie lunged, almost tumbling out of Abby's arms. The woman took Katie and hugged her close. "Momma missed you." The man at the table laughed.

"Abby, my sister Rebecca and her husband, Jack, if you haven't already realized it." Blake stood and calmly walked over to the trio. He glanced back at the table. "And this is Vanessa."

There was a coldness in Blake's voice Abby hadn't heard before. She nodded at Jack and at Vanessa, who basically looked down her nose at Abby. Nothing new. She'd seen this before with other families. She was the hired help.

"I can't thank you enough," Rebecca said. "I had no idea what happened to Mom until I called her this morning."

"We saw her yesterday, and she looks great," Abby said.

"Oh, that's nice." Rebecca nuzzled Katie, but her gaze was on her brother and filled with questions.

Abby looked at Blake, and he grinned back. Not exactly how she pictured the morning after, but again, it was just one night. It wasn't like they were in love or anything.

"Let me get some food going; I know Miss Katie here

is hungry." Abby made her way into the kitchen. Blake followed her. The coffee smelled good, but she'd wait for cup. She opened the cabinet and pulled out cereal for Katie and opened the fridge for juice.

"Not the way I planned for our morning to go," he said softly.

Abby nodded and glanced up to see Katie's parents standing close together. Vanessa sat at the table looking at her nails. Abby didn't turn when Blake came in the kitchen. He slid his arms around her waist and kissed her neck. "Later, I'll give you a proper good morning kiss."

She wanted to snap out a retort, but couldn't. Hurt flowed through her. Did he not want his family and Vanessa, the woman he'd been dating, to know about her? Abby couldn't let herself forget she was the nanny, nothing more.

In the light of day, they were from very different worlds, and she was very aware of it. Last night was the fantasy, the dream, but daylight was reality. It was time to go home.

While Rebecca fed Katie and chatted with Blake, Abby cooked a light breakfast for all of them. From the conversation, Rebecca and Jack had arrived early this morning and couldn't wait to see Katie. They'd run into Vanessa at the airport and invited her to come with them.

Abby ate a little and stayed in the kitchen but noticed while everyone else ate, Vanessa talked to Blake and no one else. Abby sighed as she packed up all of Katie's food and other items. After breakfast was finished, she loaded the dishwasher and excused herself. Once in her room, tears filled her eyes.

She was going to miss Katie, but Blake also. *Buck up. This is life, and you knew what you signed up for.* Damn it. Why did she have to go and fall for Blake Ellington anyhow? And Katie. She'd never been so taken with one of her charges. More than ever, Abby was glad she would be leaving the nanny business behind. It hurt too much, and she'd be paying for this assignment a long time.

Taking a deep breath and straightening her spine, Abby packed up Katie's clothes and her own. While she would be leaving a piece of her heart behind, her dream was waiting for her, and she needed to stay focused on that.

Abby sat down abruptly on the bed, tears spilling out. Oh Lord. She *had* fallen for Blake. How had it happened?

She shook her head, trying to clear the misery and stop crying. No dwelling on it or what could have been. Blake was a one-night encounter. She had the knowledge going in. Too bad her heart didn't agree.

She kept busy so her mind wouldn't run away with its fantasies, but she continued to blink back tears as she stripped the bed and placed the sheets in the hamper. She called the store and arranged for them to come pick up the crib, high chair, and play pen.

She would tell Walter about it, in case Blake wasn't home. Once she had nothing left to do in the bedroom, she went out into the living room. She refused to dwell on the image of Blake holding Katie.

She couldn't suppress the memory of Blake holding a dark-haired little boy. *No, don't go there.* She took a deep breath to settle her nerves and snapped her eyes open. She could get through this.

Rebecca grinned at her. "I can't believe my brother thought he could take care of Katie on his own."

"I think he could have," Abby countered. "If it hadn't been so traumatic for Katie."

"I explained about Katie's crying," Blake said.

"My baby didn't understand." Rebecca tickled her daughter under the chin.

"No, she didn't." Abby shifted on her feet. "Well, since her parents are back, I should be leaving."

Blake frowned and handed Katie to Jack as he stood.

"I've called, and they'll pick up the baby furniture today."

"Abby." Blake strode over to her. Vanessa still sat at the table glaring at not only Abby, but Katie and her parents.

"It's time." She shook her head and went back into the bedroom to grab her suitcase and backpack. Blake was standing in the doorway when she turned.

"You don't have to leave right now," he said.

"It's better I do. Katie's mom is here; it will be less stressful for Katie."

"We haven't had a chance to talk."

"There's really nothing to talk about." She stood toe to toe with him. She wasn't going to do this with his girlfriend in the next room. "We both knew I'd be leaving when it was time."

He opened his mouth to say something, and closed it.

Abby breathed in and out, trying to control her own reactions to him. She wanted to stay. She wanted him to take her back to his bed and never let her out. But it couldn't happen. She had a new job to go to, and she'd never fit into Blake's life on a permanent basis. Except, if he asked her to stay, she would. She'd let it all go for one more night in his arms. If he asked.

"I'll walk you out." He moved out of the doorway.

"No need." She swept by him, fighting tears. Abby refused to look at Vanessa; the woman would take pleasure in her misery. She'd met those types before. Rebecca was holding Katie, a slight frown on her face. "She's an angel to take care of." Abby stopped and placed a kiss on Katie's forehead before walking out of the apartment.

At the lobby, she turned in her card key, told Walter about the furniture pick-up and where the stroller was in Blake's apartment.

It wasn't until she was back in her apartment forty-five minutes later she let the tears fall.

She curled up on her sofa. There was something in the pocket of the light sweater she wore. She fished out a baby sock. Oh goodness, she'd put it there yesterday when they were visiting Blake's mother.

Arms that had been full of a baby and a man yesterday were now so empty, she could hardly lift them. She closed her eyes and rested her head against the back of the sofa. It was better this way, she assured herself.

Tomorrow, when she met with Paul at Scrumptious Addiction, she had to be on her A-game. But right now, she didn't even care.

Katie wasn't the only one who had stolen Abby's heart. Blake had too. But she couldn't have Blake. She'd allow herself this one afternoon of the what ifs, then she'd shore up her defenses.

* * * *

Blake was glad when his sister, brother-in-law, and Katie left an hour later. His sister kept asking him questions about Abby he wasn't prepared to answer. And there was Vanessa.

"Well, everyone is gone, why don't we go have brunch somewhere," she said.

"Go home, Vanessa." He wasn't in the mood to deal with her right now.

"But—"

He held up his hand. "Look, we'll talk later in the week, but I have work to do."

"Oh, very well." She gave him a kiss on the cheek which sent a chill through his body and left. Blake flopped down on the sofa.

The apartment was quiet, too quiet. He prowled around before grabbing his jacket and going for a walk.

It was as if the weather knew he was feeling miserable, because clouds had rolled in. Instead of the nice, sunny days they'd had, it was now overcast and cool. Blake walked to the park where they'd taken Katie and just stood there. Even the park was empty, just like his heart.

Why did Abby leave so abruptly? She'd seemed very uncomfortable this morning. In a way, he couldn't blame her. It wasn't the way he'd planned her wake-up. Until his sister had texted him at six this morning.

Their plane had just landed, and they were heading straight for his place since she'd talked to their mother and found out Blake had Katie at his place. Blake carried Abby to her bed, checked on Katie, and got dressed.

He hadn't expected Vanessa to be with his sister. He'd had a hard time being gracious to a woman he really wasn't interested in ever seeing again. To keep his sister entertained until Katie woke, he told her how he'd ended up babysitting and why he'd hired Abby. Rebecca had nothing but praise for Practically Perfect Nannies. She'd used them a few times when Jack was gone so she could run errands.

When Abby came out with Katie, he recognized the mask she'd put on. His first instinct was to get her alone, but he pushed down the caveman feelings. They'd made no promises to each other, but he wanted to get one out of her.

For the first time in his life, this was more than sex. He'd watched her while she slept last night. Beautiful, sexy, honest Abby. In the past week, she'd wormed her way into his life and his heart. He didn't want her to go today, but what choice did he have? She'd looked petrified he might make a scene, so he'd held the door for her—the hardest thing he'd ever done in his life.

But he could call her. Pulling out his cell phone, he punched the button. "This is Abby with Practically Perfect Nannies, I'm not available right now. Please leave a message."

Blake hung up. A company phone? How had he not known that? Maybe because he'd only texted her, not called her. Damn. He'd have to wait until tomorrow to try and reach her. But he would find her. Determination filled his veins. He wasn't going to let Abby get away from him.

* * * *

Almost two weeks later, Blake wasn't so sure he could find Abby. It was the one time his money meant nothing. On Monday, he'd called her cell again and got her voice mail, so he called the agency only to be told Abby wasn't available.

He'd gone down to the agency's office and talked with the owner. She told him they would pass on the message, but it was all they could do. It was up to Abby, and the agency wouldn't divulge her personal information. He sighed.

In desperation, he tried checking culinary schools to see if she was a student anywhere. No luck. She hadn't mentioned where her sister went to college, so he couldn't search for her. Heck, he didn't even know her sister's name. Same with her brother. What a mess.

Vanessa had called last night, wanting to see him.

Blake hadn't wanted to go out tonight, but Vanessa kept bugging him. She wanted to try a specialty restaurant she'd heard about. He'd already put Vanessa off last week. He take her for a good dinner, and he'd tell her he was off the market.

Because he was. He would find Abby. He had her name and knew she had to live in the area. A good private investigator would be able to find her.

He escorted Vanessa into the restaurant. It was busy, but they were seated right away since they had a reservation.

The décor was subtle, but not over the top. Waiters and waitresses scurried around.

"Blake, are you listening?" Vanessa's high pitch voice broke into his throughs.

"Sorry." He wasn't truly sorry, but it was the polite thing to say.

"I was asking you about the Baker Gala next month."

"I'm not going."

"But…"

"Good evening and welcome to Scrumptious Delights. I'm Wayne, your server. May I get you something to drink?"

"A glass of your finest Merlot," Vanessa said.

"Very good, ma'am. Sir?"

"I'll have the same."

"The specials tonight are wild caught salmon in a dill sauce, top sirloin with a red wine sauce, and our vegetarian selection is baked chili tofu, kale, and sesame noodles. I'll be right back with your drinks."

Blake picked up his menu. While the specials sounded good, he missed Abby's cooking. Good down to earth food. Blake shut the menu and set it down when he couldn't figure out what he wanted.

The waiter returned with their drinks and a basket of bread. Vanessa didn't even acknowledge him. "Are you ready to order?" he asked.

"I'll have a Caesar salad, dressing on the side, and steamed vegetables." Vanessa snapped her menu shut and handed it to the waiter.

Blake barely stopped himself from rolling his eyes. She was the one who wanted to try this restaurant and she orders nothing? "I'll have the top sirloin medium, with baked potato, and broccoli. As a starter I'd like to try the lasagna bites." When he read the description, they had sounded good.

"Very nice, sir. I'll bring your appetizer out first." The waiter took his menu and walked away.

Vanessa sat back in her chair. "I was hoping you would take me to the Baker Gala."

Blake let out a breath. Vanessa only had one thing on her mind. Vanessa. It was time to have the talk.

* * * *

Abby looked at the computer screen and laughed. "Who orders a salad and steamed vegetables in a restaurant called Scrumptious Addictions with so many mouth-watering items on the menu?" She'd seen a lot in her restaurant work, but this one had to take the cake in her book.

Paul laughed. "We get them all the time."

Abby shook her head and got to work. She'd met with Paul the Monday after her job with Blake was done. Not only had his pastry chef left unexpectedly but so had one of his chefs. Abby was doing double duty and loving every second of it.

Paul gave her control over the desserts, so she was

able to fix some of her favorites and some new ones, all had gone over very well. She'd been working twelve to fifteen-hour days for the last week and a half. Paul insisted the restaurant be closed on Monday's so she at least had one day off.

While she watched the order board, she also kept her eye on the other chefs, making sure they were doing their job as the sous chef had called in sick. Even as busy as she was, her thoughts always turned to Blake, especially on days like today when she made the simple chocolate filled pastry shells. The joy on his face rushed to the front of her thoughts, and her heart ached for those days.

Abby pulled the lasagna bites out of the fridge, put them in the quick cook oven, and grabbed a plate. She spread her homemade marinara sauce on the plate, and kept an eye on the countdown on the timer.

It pinged, and she pulled the perfectly cooked appetizer out of the oven and plated them. She poured heated marinara sauce in a bowl. "Appetizer ready, Wayne," she called as he walked into the serving area.

She placed the plate on the shelf along with the bowl, and Wayne grabbed it. Abby smiled. Blake would have loved those bites.

He'd called Practically Perfect Nannies looking for her. All they had told him was she wasn't available and passed on the message he wanted to speak with her. She'd received the message this last Monday when she went in to talk with her boss.

She owed it to Irene to tell her she was quitting face to face. Irene wasn't surprised. She cut Abby her last paycheck, which included the money from taking care of Katie, hugged Abby, and wished her well.

Abby hadn't looked back, even when Irene called her again to let her know Blake was looking for her, and clients were requesting her. Heck, she didn't have time. The only time the kitchen was fairly quiet was in the early morning hours as she got her desserts ready. She'd also started baking fresh rolls for dinner as well.

"Henry, watch the steak; it's medium, not medium well."

"Yes, Chef."

Chef. The word sent a shiver of happiness through her. Maybe on Monday she'd give Blake a call and see what he wanted, but what did it matter? She noticed he'd gone to some event with some woman other than Vanessa. He'd moved on and so should she.

The order was almost ready so she buzzed the waiter. It was one thing she loved about the restaurant. Paul had modernized everything. The staff wore little pager-like devices which let them know when they were needed in the kitchen. Wayne waltzed into the serving area just as the food was plated.

"The gentleman sends his compliments on the lasagna bites," Wayne said as he picked up the dinners.

"Tell him thank you." Abby turned as her name was called. Enough thinking about Blake and what could have been.

* * * *

Blake finished his dinner and sat back with a satisfied smile. The food was more than excellent, and those lasagna bites were to die for. Of course, Vanessa stuck to her salad and veggies.

He thought about Abby and how good an appetite she had. She'd admitted to him she had a sweet tooth, so walking to the park everyday helped keep her from gaining weight. Blake looked at Vanessa, *really* looked.

Her face was slightly gaunt, her color pasty, and he could see her collar bone. She didn't appeal to him at all. He wanted a woman who looked healthy and happy. Vanessa didn't. The waiter brought coffee for him and the dessert menu. Blake ordered dessert.

"Really, Blake, an appetizer and dessert?" Vanessa said. "You'll start filling out in the middle if you're not careful."

"It's my choice." He hadn't realized how annoying Vanessa was about food. She complained the entire time about what he ate. About how her salad wasn't crisp enough and the veggies overcooked.

"Vanessa," he started. "As much as I've enjoyed us dating from time to time, it's come to an end."

"Oh?"

When Wayne sat the dessert plate in front of him, a twinge of excitement went through him. The pastry shells looked familiar. He took a bite of one. Chocolate, caramel, and banana burst onto his taste buds.

Abby made these. He was sure of it. As Wayne walked by, he flagged him down. "Is it possible I can complement the pastry chef on these personally?"

"I'll ask, sir." Wayne walked away.

"Come on, Blake, it's just chocolate," Vanessa whined.

"It's more than that." He ate more of the dessert and looked up when a man approached the table. His heart sank.

"I'm Paul, the owner. My pastry chef is gone for the night."

Disappointment flared in Blake's gut. "I wanted to compliment her on the dessert. I've not tasted anything like it." Partial truth. He was sure Abby was the pastry chef.

Paul's eyes widened. "I'll let her know. Have a wonderful evening."

At least Blake had confirmation the chef was a woman. It had to be Abby, but if she was already gone for the night…or was she? He saw more desserts come out of the kitchen. Maybe he'd sit here for a while.

"Are you not done, yet?" Vanessa asked.

"No. Look, Vanessa, you're a nice woman"—maybe for a barracuda—"but we're over."

Vanessa huffed out a breath, threw her napkin on the table, and stood. "There was too much butter on those steamed vegetables. I need to work it off. I'll catch a cab to the Rocket Club. You can find me there when you change your mind."

"I won't change my mind." He was sure of that.

Blake watched Vanessa storm out of the restaurant with a sense of relief. Now, maybe he could enjoy his dessert and coffee in peace. He'd hang out until the restaurant closed to see if Abby was here. It wasn't he didn't believe the owner, but he also knew they protected their staff. And the owner had no way of knowing whether he was here to poach the staff.

* * * *

Abby leaned against the counter as the kitchen cleanup began. There wasn't a lot of it; they cleaned as they cooked, but now the night was over. There were some stragglers in the dining room, but they'd already been told the restaurant was closing.

"Hey, Abby," Wayne said. "The gentlemen at table ten is asking for you again."

"I gave him the standard line, told him you were gone," Paul said.

She wiped her hands on her apron. "I guess this once

I can go out. No one has been this persistent."

"Remember you're mine," Paul said. "I'm not losing you."

"I'm happy here." Abby followed Wayne out of the kitchen. The dining room was almost empty. There was a couple sitting in one of the booths and a man…Blake! She stopped in her tracks and stared at him.

Blake looked up, and a smile formed on his lips as he stood. Abby didn't move as he walked over to her. "I knew it had to be you." He took her hands in his.

"How?" was all she could get out.

"Dessert. You made it for me, and I'll never forget the unique blend of flavors. Come sit with me for a minute. Please." He guided her toward the table.

Abby didn't know what to think. What was he doing here? He pulled a chair out for her, and she sat without thinking. That's when she noticed the second plate on the table. "Where's your date?"

"Gone, thank goodness." He moved his chair to be close to her. "I left a message with the nanny agency."

"I know. I got it this last Monday."

"And you didn't call me back?" There was

disappointment in his voice.

"What do we have to say to each other, Blake?"

He stared at her. "A lot." He took her hands in his again. "I'm sorry Sunday morning didn't work out the way I wanted it to. My plan was to wake you with a kiss and coffee, and if Katie cooperated, a shower together, and the breakfast I planned on cooking for you."

"You were going to cook for me?" Her heart opened a crack.

"Yes. It wouldn't have been anything fancy, scrambled eggs and toast. But my sister showed up with Vanessa."

"I won't lie. I was hurt, Blake. Not by your sister, but by the other woman being in your apartment. A place you said no other women but family had been. I wasn't sure how to act, so I went back into nanny mode."

"I understand why you retreated, but I didn't invite Vanessa to my place. She came with my sister." He paused. "I'm sorry about the whole screwup. You left, and I didn't know where you went. I have an appointment with a private investigator on Monday."

"What?"

"I was determined to find you. Someone was looking out for me when I walked in here tonight."

"With a date," she reminded him.

"I have no interest in Vanessa. In fact, I told her. The only woman I'm interested in is sitting right in front of me."

She shook her head, but she couldn't deny the warmth his words sent through her blood stream.

"Oh yes." He released her hands and framed her cheeks with his palms. "Will you give me a chance? Will you give us a chance?"

"But…"

"What?"

"Blake, you could have any woman you want. I'm a nothing."

"You're not a nothing. You're Abby. My Abby."

The crack in her heart widened. "How long will I be your Abby?"

"As long as you'll have me or until I can put a wedding ring on your finger and keep you for life."

The crack in her heart stitched itself together at those words. "I won't give up my job."

"Of course not. I said it the entire time you took care of Katie. You are a fantastic cook, I mean, chef, and you deserve to do what you want."

"What about your playboy ways?"

Blake laughed. "Gossip rags exaggerate everything. Haven't you learned anything about me? Yes, I've gone out with a lot of women, but you're the one who's been in my bed, not them."

Her eyes widened. "It wasn't just a line?"

"No. And until Vanessa on Sunday, no other woman has been in my apartment except family. I know the papers make it sound like I'm sleeping with everyone I take on a date, but it's simply not true. A lot of those dates are to charity functions, and while I can go without a date, it looks much better if I have one."

"And you're saying you've never slept with any of them?"

"I wish I could say I hadn't, but I've never taken them to my bed or to my apartment. It was a rule I never broke, until you."

"I don't know what to say."

"Say you'll give us a chance. I really want to explore

what we have together."

"It was just one night."

"It was more. From the moment you walked into my apartment, I knew you were different. Please, Abby. You know me. The real me. Please trust me with your heart."

Abby blinked as tears came to her eyes.

"For God's sake, put the man out of his misery so we can all go home," Paul said. Abby turned her head to see Paul and the kitchen staff standing there.

She nodded. "Yes, I'll try."

Blake let out a shout and gathered her into his arms as he stood. "You'll never want to leave me."

Epilogue

Abby put the finishing touches on dinner as her stomach churned. In the past two months, she and Blake had been almost inseparable. Now they were having his family over for dinner.

He walked into the kitchen and put his arms around her waist. "Would you quit fussing?"

"I want this to be perfect."

"It is." He kissed her temple. "You've met my family before."

"Yes…" The doorbell rang, and she jumped.

"Breathe," He released her and opened the door.

"Abab," Katie cried out, reaching for Abby.

Abby took Katie from her mother's arms. "You remember me, do you?"

Rebecca laughed. "I hope you left all the baby proofing on the tables; this one is fast on her feet."

Abby put Katie down, and she took off at a run with her parents following behind. When Abby straightened,

Maggie was smiling. "So good to see you again, Abby."

They hugged, and Abby's nerves quieted. These were good people. Blake put his arm around her as his mother made her way into the living room with barely any limp.

Family. They came in all sizes and all shapes. Abby was glad she fit into this one. It was time for her to let go of her life with her mother. In three months, her brother and sister were coming for a visit to meet Blake.

A new family.

Life couldn't get better.

Thank you for reading *Temporary Nanny for the Tycoon*. If you enjoyed this book, please consider leaving a review on Goodreads, or your retailer's website, and know that it would be greatly appreciated. For new release information and news about Marie Tuhart, please join her newsletter.

Bio:

Marie Tuhart lives in the beautiful Pacific Northwest. Marie loves to read and write. When she's not writing, she spends time with her two dogs, Tommy and Trina, family, traveling, and enjoying life.

Marie is a multi-published author with The Wild Rose Press, Trifecta Publishing and self-publishing.

Other books by Marie Tuhart

Tempt (Wicked Sanctuary Series)

Entice (Wicked Sanctuary Series)

Seduce (Wicked Sanctuary Series)

Ravish (Wicked Sanctuary Series)

Possess (Wicked Sanctuary Series)

Tantalize (Wicked Sanctuary Series)

Astrology Anthology: Aries and Leo

Edged (Wicked Sanctuary Series) Spring 2023

Go to Marie's website for all list of all her published books.

PREVIEW OF *EDGED*

Kaley Clark parked her Fluff and Puff van outside the house, surprised when her client, Clara Pierce, wasn't outside waiting for her. That was unusual. Kaley got out and smiled, proud of the decal wrap on her van. Dogs, cats, and contact information in a park setting covered the sides, back, and top. It had cost her a pretty penny, but she loved it.

Tapping the springer spaniel leaping through the air in the picture, Kaley secured her shoulder length auburn hair and made her way to the front door, hoping Clara was all right. Nugget, Clara's Maltipoo, barked, reassuring Kaley.

The door opened and…Kaley took a step back.

Anthony, or Payne as they called him in the club, stood there, his black hair mussed, and his blue eyes dazed.

Her heart sped up. Sexy didn't begin to describe this man. "Can I help you?" His deep voice sent shivers up her spine.

"I'm—"

"It's Kaley. Let her in, Anthony. Remember? She's here to groom Nugget."

"You're the dog groomer?"

Kaley bit the inside of her lower lip so she didn't smile. "I don't know why everyone seems surprised to find out I'm the dog groomer."

"Maybe because you'd make the perfect model for painting," he said, holding the door open so she could enter.

"I don't think so." She laughed off his comment. Kaley was aware she was average looking, nothing special.

"I'm in the family room, dear. Don't let my grandson distract you," Clara's voice rang out strong and clear.

"Is she okay?" Kaley asked in a low voice.

"Sprained ankle. She's been told to stay off of it." He shut the door as Kaley walked down the small hallway. Nugget started whining and wiggling when she saw Kaley. "Hi Clara," she said, seeing the woman sitting with her leg propped up on a pillow, trying to hold on to the energetic dog.

"Allow me," Anthony said, maneuvering around her to remove the baby gate across the doorway. "We're trying to keep Nugget confined to this room."

"I see." Kaley slipped by him and swore she smelled paint and turpentine. If she remembered right, Anthony was an artist. He also did demos at Wicked Sanctuary. Kaley's heart pounded with thoughts about all the times she'd watched his intense sessions, never sure she was up for his brand of play. Deep down, some feral part of her wanted to step up and try, though she'd never had the courage.

Nugget jumped out of Clara's arms and launched herself at Kaley. "Easy, Nugget." Kaley caught the dog as she jumped into her arms. Laughter bubbled up as she was given doggy kisses all over her face.

"Nugget," Clara admonished.

"It's fine," Kaley said, tightening her arms around Nugget so the small dog didn't fall. "Are you in pain, Clara? I could have done this on another day."

"It's nothing." Clara waved her hands. "Doctor's being cautious."

"Doctor is making sure you heal," Anthony said, giving Clara a pointed look.

Kaley's knees weakened. There it was, that Dom stare. Oh yes, she'd seen him around Wicked Sanctuary, and she'd kept her distance. He seemed a little too intense for her, but that didn't stop her lady bits from taking notice.

"The usual?" she asked Clara. She was here to groom the dog, not make eyes at Anthony, no matter what her body said.

"Oh yes, dear. That would be wonderful."

"All right. I'll ring the bell when I'm done." Kaley turned.

"I'll walk you out," Anthony said, putting his hand on her elbow.

Tingles flowed from her elbow throughout her body. This wasn't fair. She didn't want to react to him this way but couldn't seem to control herself.

He opened the door for her. "Do you need anything?" he asked.

"Just Nugget."

"Shame," he whispered. "Maybe when you're done with Nugget I can have a moment of your time?"

She frowned. "Why?"

His grin caused her heart hit high gear again.

"To talk."

"Talk?" Now she sounded like a parrot. "I'm not sure we have anything to talk about."

"I think we might."

Kaley shook her head and walked to her van. Nope. Not going to happen. He already tilted her equilibrium, and she wasn't model material no matter what he thought.

* * * *

Anthony Pierce watched the pretty dog groomer hurry to her van. Fluff and Puff. He grinned as he closed the door. Kaley seemed familiar to him, while her business name wasn't. He could have seen her or met her around town.

Maybe at his gallery opening. The opening had been filled with people. Not his favorite thing. He disliked cloying crowds, but he had to keep up appearances, so he'd done the opening. A grin slid over his lips. Kaley may have laughed off his comment about her being his model, but he wasn't kidding. He wanted to paint her.

"How long will the grooming take?" he asked his

grandmother.

"About an hour." Clara picked up her book.

"Okay, I'm going to go back and paint for a bit." The image of Kaley was implanted in his head, and he was itching to put her into his latest work.

"Go."

Making his way to the sunroom, which had become his temporary workspace, Anthony glanced at his work. When his grandmother sprained her ankle, the doctor said she needed to stay off of it until it healed, which could be up to two weeks.

Anthony had immediately moved into the main house with her. There was a cottage on his grandmother's property he'd lived in since he was eighteen, when his parents threw him out. He shook his head, unwilling to give much thought to that time in his life. He'd been confused and set adrift. Luckily, his grandmother took him in and gave him the time to come into himself.

Stepping inside the sunroom, he put a new canvas on the stand and began sketching. His muse took over, and his fingers tingled at being back at work again. Between the gallery opening and the club, he hadn't had much time to paint. He picked up some charcoal and began sketching the chaise lounge in his mind. Anthony's body heated as an image of a woman started to form.

An unusual reaction when he was sketching. It was Kaley. Something about her pulled at him. Once she was finished with Nugget, they would talk. He wanted her as his model, and it was the first time in a very long time he wanted to spend time with a woman.